AF535138

TWO CLOSE

a story of survival

Cover Photograph Cheriecokeley | Dreamstime.com/43955499

Roberta M. Roy Photograph by Lorna Tychostup

Book & Cover Design by Elliot Toman

Map by Roberta M. Roy

Soft Cover ISBN: 978-1-938729-93-5

ePub Edition ISBN: 978-1-938729-58-4

ePDF Edition ISBN: 978-1-938729-59-1

Published by:

Alva Press, Inc., 250 Beechwood Avenue 23A

Poughkeepsie, NY 12601

SAN 256-6915

http://alvapressinc.com

TWO CLOSE

a story of survival

Roberta M Roy

ALVA PRESS
Poughkeepsie, New York

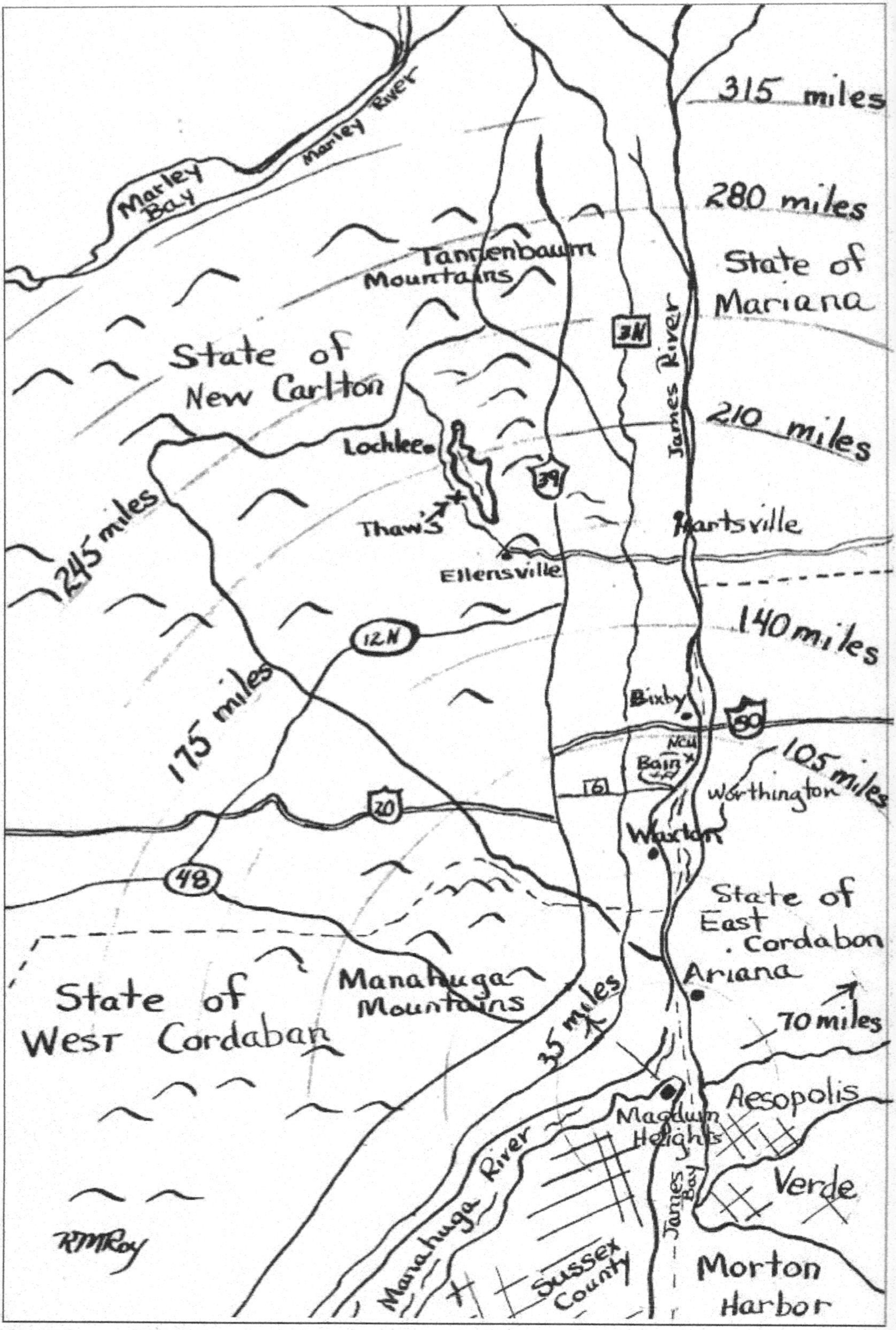

Marley River
Marley Bay
315 miles
280 miles
State of Mariana
Tannenbaum Mountains
3N
State of New Carlton
James River
210 miles
Lochlee
39
Thaw's
Hartsville
245 miles
Ellensville
140 miles
12N
175 miles
Bixby
80
NCU
Bain
105 miles
16
Worthington
20
Waxton
48
State of East Cordabon
Ariana
Manahuga Mountains
State of West Cordaban
70 miles
35 miles
Aesopolis
Magdum Heights
Manahuga River
James Bay
Verde
RMRoy
Sussex County
Morton Harbor

TABLE OF CONTENTS

Preface

Jolt: a rural noir, the prequel to *Two Close: A Story of Survival*, follows the events in the lives of the inhabitants of Lochlee, a village tucked in the mountains of North Country in the American state of New Carlton, two hundred miles north of the sight of a nuclear meltdown at Magdum Heights Nuclear Power Plant. Because of the influx of forced immigrants from the areas threatened by its resultant radioactive fallout, the village is overwhelmed by their numbers ... all in need of food, water, clothing, and housing. As a result, independent of FEMA and the Red Cross, both of which have been overwhelmed, the villagers establish a Point of Distribution (POD) and provide supplies and medical care for the newcomers, including those with radiation sickness; also, the emigres establish a small shanty town on the shore of Lake Lochlee.

Thus, in Jolt: *a rural noir* we witnessed the successful efforts of the Lochlee villagers to support and provide for the emigres. Some of these emigres had been introduced and followed from the meltdown to their settlement in Locklee. Four of those introduced, however, disappeared from the story. They were the Matters' family, Mary, and Lou the parents and their sons, Jason, aged 13, and Marty aged 10. *Two Close: A Story of Survival* follows this family's lives after the nuclear meltdown.

Mary and Lou have been affected by the explosion of nearby radioactive dirty bombs while their sons have gone on the road to avoid the fallout from The Plant. And as given the electrical grid to their home is down, they sons are unable to contact their parents to confirm that they are even alive. The boys left their home as Jason, the older son, previously coached by his father as to whether in the event of a meltdown to hunker down or flee, decided that he and Marty should take off before any fallout could reach them. Mary and Lou, however, are less lucky, and the dirty bombs that explode near them cause Mary to be sprayed with radioactive matter and Lou to be seriously injured and to suffer amnesia. As such, in addition to their parents being separated from each other, so, too, are the boys separated from their parents. *Two Close: A Story of Survival* traces the events in their lives over the next year to the four of them in their efforts to survive, heal, and reunite.

ONE Lenore and Mary

April 12 to April 30, 2018

Lenore's family had been first to move into the development, the Matters, the second. With Lenore's parents divorced, remarried, and moved out of state, they visited rarely. Lenore and Carlos, Lenore's Puerto Rican husband, had known Mary and Lou since early in their marriages and the two families were remarkably close.

Lenore remembered the feeling of anticipation watching from behind slanted blinds as Mary, Lou, and Jason, their older son, toured the property with the man Lenore recognized as being the Morning Glory Heights developer and then later, the kick of seeing the Allied truck barrel down the newly paved road and pull up in front of the new house, only to be followed soon thereafter by a sedan transporting Lou, Mary, and Jason who at that time was yet a preschooler, possibly a year or so older than Lenore's Ricky.

Lenore thought of how if her Ricky was now almost twelve, Jason must be near fourteen and Marty probably ten. Gosh, she missed them. Lenore could not imagine how difficult the Magdum Heights event had been for Mary. And poor Lou.

But enough of the maudlin—Lenore was recalling earlier days: The truck had arrived and so too, the Matters. So, Lenore had hoisted Ricky into her arms and trundled over to say hello. Figuring they would soon need a breather from the settling-in process, Lenore invited them all to come over for tea or coffee and when Mary and Jason arrived at her door, Lenore's spirits soared.

There was pretty Mary, her bobbed wavy blond hair having charmingly lost its orderly look and accented by perspiration-soaked tendrils was plastered about her forehead and cheeks. As for Jason, he headed straight for Ricky's stroller which Lenore used when Ricky's legs would no longer hold him as he made his way from one piece of furniture to the next and it was time for a bottle.

So much for nap time on that day! The two young mothers laughed and talked, and the boys played peek-a-boo and magic until Ricky was too tired to laugh anymore—a reality even Jason recognized, and he joined the women at the table for milk and cookies. Ricky went back to his bottle, eyes, and ears not about to miss a trick.

And so, began a friendship that would in time include their husbands, their first sons, and, after their birth, their second ones.

When the boys grew older and entered school, Mary took a position as a speech language pathologist in Aesopolis, and Lenore went to work as a special education teacher. Mary's job was some miles south of Morning Glory Heights in the large city district of Aesopolis. Lenore worked in a small city twenty miles north of Ariana and just a bit south of Waxton. Like Waxton, it was also on the other side of the James River. It would have been too far to commute except for the fact that both mornings and evenings she drove against traffic, so it was a rare day that it took her more than half an hour. Also, as luck would have it, Sandra, the boys' babysitter, lived on this side of the James, just before the Narrows Bridge and only another five miles north of Morning Glory Heights, so still within the school district and where the boys could be dropped off from their buses after school and Lenore could pick them up on the way home from work.

And so, it was that the four boys grew up together: First there were Jason and Ricky. Then came Marty. And then, just about the time Marty started school, came Stephen. And at the end of Lenore's maternity leave, Stephen joined the others at Sandra's in the after school program she ran at her house and from which, for lack of a better plan, both boys continued in until Ricky reached the age of twelve and Stephen was five and in kindergarten. At that point Lenore found a mother in Morning Glory Heights who was still home with her baby and could keep an eye on her two boys' mornings before school and after school until Lenore arrived home.

So on that fateful day when The Plant went down, Mary was in Acropolis, Marty and Jason at home in Ariana, Ricky and Stephen with Sandra, Carlos on a building contract just south of Bain, Lou at The Plant, and Lenore at work on the other side of the river.

And so, it was that all their stories varied.

On her way to meet her husband Lou for lunch at the Magdum Heights Power Plant where he worked, Mary Matters stopped for gum in a small, well frequented plaza. As she opened her car door to descend, something exploded nearby. Given her knowledge of terrorism tactics and with her husband working at the nuclear power plant, her lips formed the words "Dirty bomb." And she was right. The explosion had occurred close enough that the left side of her body was hit by flying debris and some of the radioactive ash from the bomb spattered her left arm, irradiating it.

Mary slammed closed the car door and grabbed wipes from a plastic container she kept on her seat for quick clean-ups. From discussions with Lou, she knew she had to remove if possible, all the radioactive matter if she were to avoid radiation sickness. She scrubbed her arm quickly with one after another sheet. Clean enough. She would shower when she reached home. She started the car and backed out quickly in the direction away from the site of the explosion. Moments away, she slammed on the brakes, rolled down the driver-side window, grabbed the used wipes, tossed them out of the window, grabbed a few more, gave her hands and arm one more thorough scrub, threw those wipes out the window, and pulled off for home. Her plan was to beat any gridlock that might occur due to any emergency and by so doing, permit her to drive the thirty miles without incident. Mary was not a worrier, but she needed to be with the boys.

Still, at the next turn off, Mary pulled off the main road, stopped, ran quickly to the trunk, almost tearing off her clothes as she went . . . anything to rid herself of the radioactive materials likely to be covering her. She knew the go-box was in the trunk and in it were flip-flops and a sweat suit.

Several cars passed her. They did not stop for the woman tearing off her clothes and shoes. Nor did they stop when, stark naked, she opened the box in the trunk, pulled out an over-sized sweatshirt and donned it. Next were the sweatpants. Then the flip-flops.

Grabbing a large ice scraper with cleaning brush that was kept there regardless of the season, Mary ran around the car and swept off any ash she found on the top of the car, being careful in the process to avoid having it blow or be swept onto her clothes. Also, she cleaned the cracks at the bottom of the windows. She then threw the scraper far from the road into the bushes, and leaving her clothes where they had fallen, slammed shut the trunk, and continued her way home.

Mary was in survival mode now. She recalled the automatic car wash about five minutes away. It was run by a guy who lived in a nearby trailer. The town had been working to force him into upgrading the looks of the place but the problem was, they couldn't find any safety or health violations and he had been there so long any changes in the statutes since he opened the place had no effect. He had been grandfathered in on them all.

He ran his trailer on solar panels which he balanced with the effects of geothermal cooling that he had rigged up in the stream that ran beside the place. He even had a way of keeping his water bill down by storing and recycling some of the water he used in the car wash. For emergency situations he used a solar powered, battery run generator. Many saw him as a real kook.

If she were lucky, the generator would be working and the car wash open.

Mary's purse was still on the floor where she had thrown it when the bomb went off. A five . . . she needed a five. She pulled into the car-wash drive. The owner must have seen her coming. Probably he had been watching from the window of the trailer. They exchanged brief hellos as he lifted the long locks of his hair from his left shoulder, tossed them backward and down his back, accepted the five, and pushed a button beside the door to the carwash.

An abbreviated tootle-loo wave to the man and Mary rolled up her window. The aluminum and glass door rose. She drove in. The lights within blinked for her to stop, then go, then stop, go, stop. She did as she was expected. The car was quickly soaped, rinsed, and air blown. The aluminum and glass back door opened. The process was complete. She could feel safe again.

As she drove, in the distance she heard an explosion of sorts rock the area near Magdum Heights. Shortly thereafter, her car stalled but as luck would have it, she was able to restart it and continue her way. On arrival home some twenty minutes later, it occurred to Mary that she had no recollection whatsoever of the drive, any lights, or any other cars. Outside her own thoughts, the last thing she could visualize was the door of the carwash rising. Also, the sound of the explosion near the Plant loomed large.

After her shower, she would next locate the boys. She could not think of them now. All her years as a clinician had taught her to prioritize . . . and to wait. She had to care for herself first. A sick or dead mother would not be much good to her sons. And Jason would keep them both safe until they were together again. Once Lenore had read that in a mass event each person can only experience what they experience with everything else having an over there quality. From that, two aspects of large events emerged. The first that happened—and persisted—was the sense that what was happening was only happening here and so being of a smaller dimension, it was to be more readily understood. The second that occurred was the realization that one does not really know what is happening—although in the heat of surviving, this may not really hit home until one picks up the phone and dials and no one answers the ring tone or the charged cell phone for lack of functioning towers that work. And so, on the day the nuclear power plant . . . The Plant . . . went down not only were they all affected differently, it would in fact be months before they really could put the facts together to achieve the kind of closure similar to that which a child seeks when he does not know his parentage or when one is fired and doesn't know why.

For Lenore, she was among the lucky ones. The school day had zapped her and she rode home in silence in the effort to put all the ragged edges of a child's unexpected raging into some kind of a perspective and to figure out what she as his clinician might have done or should now do differently in the class and with him. The traffic north seemed oddly heavier than usual, but nothing more. Sandra met her at the door which was not usual. The boys were ready, light jackets on and backpacks in hand.

"Terrorism, Lenore!"

"What do you mean, Sandra?"

Ricky, who held Stephen tightly by the hand, she pushed forward with her left hand as she grasped Lenore's left hand tightly in her right. Her eyes held Lenore's. "Terrorism!" she exclaimed again.

"Sandra. Calm yourself. Where? What kind?"

"You need to call Carlos. You need to make a plan. The Plant is down. Many of the lines are down. The area around it for five to fifteen miles could be affected. You need to try your cell phone. I think the electric grid is gone. But you said Carlos was in Bain, no? Maybe you can reach him."

As Lenore reached for her cell phone, it rang. It was Carlos. Carlos had served in the Iraq War. Unlike Sandra, he understood that The Plant going down would mean radioactivity spreading around it as much as ten to thirteen miles not to mention the possibility of radioactive ash drifting above them and falling down irradiating the area for a period of seventy two hours or so . . . and this might occur within as little as a half hour. He said they didn't have to worry about radioactivity as their house was more than thirty miles from the plant and the best that could be determined was that any immediate radioactivity outside the ten mile radius at most would be due to dirty bombs. So, if she could wend her way home, she was to take the boys and go there and he would be there as soon as possible; he was on his way now. He further clarified that it was terrorism, not war and probably for now, this would be it. And they were to stay inside as the wind might bring some fallout, but that would not before perhaps thirty minutes or more.

So, Lenore took the boys and headed home. Traffic north was bumper to bumper. However, except for a few holdups at intersections where the traffic lights on secondary roads did not function, the trip home was uneventful. Carlos arrived soon after their arrival.

"Carlos!" Lenore hugged him hard. "What do we do?"

Ricky somehow hugged them both, and Stephen hugged Carlos' leg.

Carlos wrapped his right arm around his wife and older son and Stephen hugged his waist. Carlos gave a shrug. "We hunker down."

"What do you mean?"

"We stay inside. Seventy-two hours." "But the terrorists! The fallout."

"Remember how I told you how a plant is not the same as an Atomic Bomb. That when one goes down it does not make a Hiroshima?"

"What about Chernobyl?"

"If the Plant went down it too would not be like Chernobyl?"

"How can we be sure?"

"It has a different design. It will not blow out. Its overhead will drop down into the silo to shut down. If anything, it will cause fission that could affect the area nearby. But there will be no significant plume . . . no significant smoke plume of radioactive filled ash. We're at least thirty-five miles from The Plant. The likelihood of the ionizing radiation reaching us in significant amounts this far is next to nil. And if we hunker down for seventy-two hours by staying inside and drinking only our bottled water, we should be okay."

Lenore recalled what Carlos had taught her about ionizing radiation. That it would likely spew forth from a nuclear power plant that imploded. That it could be spread by the ash that came from the plant and was blown by the wind as far as two hundred miles but most significantly up to thirty miles. That the key was to either hunker down or stay inside with distance and walls between you and the ash outside for a period of seventy two hours or, if you decided there was time before fall out arrived, you could run. Carlos said they were safe to hunker down so hunker down they would. They would go to the windowless central area of the basement and stay away from the walls and windows of the basement's outer walls. They would only drink bottled water that they had stored there. And eat canned goods. For seventy-two hours. In that manner they would avoid being irradiated by the ionizing radiation from any fall out and by so doing, avoid at some later date, becoming victims of the cancer such irradiation might cause.

"Whoa-okay. Whoa-okay. We need some action now." Carlos thought that keeping the boys involved would lessen their worry.

"Action?"

"Yes. Just to be sure, we need a leaf bag. Remember we have some downstairs in our Hideaway House?"

"I'll get one, Dad." And Ricky was gone.

"Mommy, I'm hungry."

"First things first, son," said Carlos.

"Lenore, take the boys to the bathroom, have them strip and shower. You, too. They should put their clothes in the leaf bag. I will get rid of it later."

"What are we doing?"

"It probably isn't necessary, but we are deconning. Just in case some radioactive ash has reached any of us. That's also why we are staying in the house. Downstairs. And not going out for seventy-two hours. In case of ionizing radiation. We are staying in to keep any ash from getting on us—any fallout. And we are only eating canned and bottled foods. Or foods from the fridge before the loss of electricity turns it bad in the heat. Everything else goes out. Mostly to make the point. Remember. Only canned, bottled, or food that has been in the refrigerator."

Lenore left to get a change of clothes for each of the boys.

"Sneakers, too, into the bag. When you've showered and dressed, find something else for your feet. Then everybody downstairs. If you have any special toy you want to bring with you, take it when you go. You won't be up for three days. Done. No ifs, buts, ands, or ors."

Even Stephen put aside his want of food.

After the boys . . . under Carlos's supervision in the main bathroom . . . and Lenore and then Carlos had showered . . . in the one off their bedroom, and they all had changed their clothes—including their shoes, the boys and Lenore headed for the basement while Carlos collected his family's castoff clothes and any food sitting around. Walking under his golf umbrella, Carlos then transported everything to the large plastic trash bins. When Carlos came back inside, as he passed the threshold of the door, he tossed the flip-flops he had been wearing off the side of the steps and stood the golf umbrella just outside the door. Then he joined the rest of his family downstairs for what was to be the longest three days of their lives.

Lenore brought down with her bread and cold cuts from the refrigerator and a carton of milk. They opened and sat on the sleeping bags there and shared the picnic lunch makings and talked.

“So, Dad, how long do we have to stay down here?” It was Ricky. He was twelve and generally quiet, but he had a way of getting to the facts fast.

“Seventy-two hours.”

“Will we have to stay after dark, too?” asked five-year-old Stephen.

“We'll be sleeping here for three nights. So, you might as well settle in for the long haul,” answered Carlos.

“But why, Dad?”

“Well, Stephen, it's just a ‘just in case’ measure. Just in case there is fall out with radioactivity that comes.”

“Radiumactivity?”

“Radi-O-activity,” corrected Ricky.

“Radi-O-activity. Okay?” Stephen was a little impatient at being corrected.

“Where's it come from?” asked Ricky.

“Well, there is a chance that there might be some ash that came out from the plant when it went down, and the wind might have blown it towards us.”

“Yeah.”

“And that ash might have radioactivity in it.” “How can you tell?”

“Well, ever heard of a Geiger counter?”

“Grace down the street has a book called *Miss Pickerell and the Geiger Counter*. It was her grandmother's. She said it was kinda' interesting. And old."

"Well, a Geiger counter or dosimeter as it is also called, measures how much radiation there is near it. But there is always a little radiation around us, just not enough to bother us. X-Rays also give off radiation. So does the sun."

"What's radiation?"

"Well, radiation is something you can't see, or smell and you can't tell it is there. But if there is radioactive ash, you might be able to see the ash. Except the ash could be so small, you don't see it. But if you are near it and there is enough of it you can get radiation sickness."

"So, are we going to get sick?" Ricky asked.

"No. Probably not. But just to be sure, we are staying in the house for three days," Carlos held up three fingers and looked directly at Stephen, "and three," he paused and moved his raised hand forward a bit to emphasize the number, "nights."

"Why?"

"Well, Stephen, if the ash . . . the fallout comes . . . it may be radioactive and most of the radioactivity lasts for three days . . . at least the danger does. So, we are staying inside and downstairs as that radioactivity can even come through walls."

"Wow!" Stephen shuttered.

"But not to worry." Carlos gave Stephen a hug. "Right, Ricky?" He gave his older son a thumbs up.

"Right, Dad." Somehow, he could not return the thumbs up. It was all a little too scary for him. He didn't even know what questions to ask.

* * *

As luck would have it, the weather held, and in the days, sunlight streamed through the basement windows, and they used their can openers and except for Carlos' quick runs for forgotten essentials, they ate, slept, talked, played, quarreled, and took care of their bodily needs in the Hideaway Room located for reasons they could only guess, central to the basement with a door that opened to the east side of the house.

It came to Lenore that this was why Carlos had stocked it so carefully—with everything from twenty gallons of water to cans of tuna and corned beef to a myriad of first aid supplies and four sleeping bags. And a chamber pot. He had told them they could never know when a hurricane or tornado might come, and they would need a hideout until the storm had passed.

Lenore blushed to think how dumb it had been to have believed the sincerity of his reasons. But then she had simply chalked up all that talk of hurricanes and tornados to his having grown up in Puerto Rico and the Midwest and only since just before they had met having moved to the East Coast. Still, how kind of him not to have worried her. Just figure it. What were the chances of terrorism hitting there? Or a nuclear meltdown?

Well, now she knew.

* * *

The house was quiet. After the bomb had exploded, although Mary believed she had gotten off all the gunk she could prior to changing into the sweat suit, Mary also knew it was critical that she shower to remove any last bit of radioactive material from her arm or anywhere else it may have spattered. "Jason!" No answer. "Marty!" Silence. She turned on the shower, stripped, and suds up a face cloth and washed her face and arms first. Her hair was already wet, and the shampoo foamed reassuringly. She rinsed her hair and scrubbed the rest of herself, rinsing well before turning off the warm flow of water, drying herself, bundling her clothes in a clean towel, and tossing the resultant ball out the bedroom window. She then dressed quickly in clothes she pulled from the bedroom drawers and closet, put on a clean pair of sneakers. She confirmed the boys' bikes were gone. In the kitchen a sticky note read, "We saw the glow of fires. Marty and I are headed north. Will contact you when I can. Jason."

Mary's knees went weak beneath her. The boys gone. Who knew where? Or how to contact them?

She tried the phone. Not working. And their battery-run radio. Static. Definitely more than dirty bombs. The Plant was down and with it the grid. Should she stay or go? It took but a split second to make the decision. She would not be able to locate the boys. It was possible Lou was not at The Plant when it went down. He could be there any minute. She would stay. There was food and water in basement. She would wait the seventy-two hours before going out. Yes, she would hunker down. And she would hope.

Downstairs in the center room, the time passed slowly. The batteries on the lights held so she was not in darkness. In the daylight hours, light streamed in from the downstairs windows. And there were books to read. And canned foods to eat. And water to drink. There also were pads and pencils and pens. The radio signal did not come back, but periodically she gave it some turns to charge the battery and tried it. Static only. The first day she felt all right and passed the time speculating as to where her sons were and imagining ways Jason kept them both safe. And in between, she tried to read and slept. The second day she felt some nausea and lacked energy. She suspected it to be the beginning of radiation sickness. Even just eating and drinking took more energy than she had. At least if the boys had left immediately, they were clear of radiation fall out. By the third day she knew she needed help. Her energy level was so low, just opening a bottle of water was a challenge. She imagined the boys checked into a motel and swimming in the indoor pool. She could not even think of Lou. That was too much. He might have been at the plant. By the afternoon of the fourth day, she would leave. She would find Lenore. Lenore would keep her hydrated as she passed through the worst of the radiation sickness. And feed her. Thank goodness Lou had put the cash there for the boys to take and that Jason had known enough to not forget to take it. Somehow, she was sure Lenore and her family would have stayed, too. Carlos would have told them there was no need for them to flee. Just wait the seventy-two hours.

* * *

Mary grabbed three bottles of water. Even they were heavy for her. Laboriously she climbed the stairs. The late afternoon light slanted downward through the front door window. She turned the knob. Her knees were weak but held her weight. She crossed the lawns and rapped on Lenore's door. "Please let them be home."

It was the late afternoon of the first day they were no longer in the Hideaway Room, so Carlos and Lenore were cleaning and straightening it. The boys were in the dining room playing War when Ricky saw Mary Matters coming up the front step. She knocked on the front door. Ricky opened the door. "Hi, Mary. You okay?"

"Hi, Ricky. Not really. Is your mother here?"

Lenore came from the living room. "Mary! What's happened?"

"I was sprayed with some radioactive gunk. From a dirty bomb. Three days ago. I'm clean, but I have radiation sickness. If I go home, can you bring me food and water until it passes? The main thing is to keep me hydrated. I'm pretty low on energy and I'm not sure the worst has hit."

"What about the boys?" "They went north."

"Oh, Mary! Come in. Come into the guest room. We'll sort everything out there. I just thought you all had fled the meltdown. I didn't see Lou's car, so I figured . . . I didn't know you were home! Where's Lou?"

"I don't know." Mary began to sob.

"Oh, Mary." Lenore held her to her, but Mary pushed her back.

"I may be radioactive. I don't think so but best to stay the distance."

Lenore decided not to ask about Jason and Marty.

Carlos came into the room. "Mary. Good to see you. I've been wondering about you all."

"Hello, Carlos."

Taking in the situation, Carlos made the decision to ask if there was anything he might do. If Lenore or Mary said no, he would leave the room and query Lenore about the situation later. "Can I help?"

Lenore answered, "No, we're okay. Maybe check on Stephen."

Lenore settled Mary into the bed in the guest room and brought her water with a straw in it and fixed her some soup which she fed to her as she lay propped up on pillows. Mary had no inclination to eat but she was not nauseous, and she knew she had to if she were to keep up her strength. Between mouthfuls Mary shared what she knew about Lou and the boys which as it turned out was just the direction in which the boys had fled and about Lou, nothing.

Lenore could not imagine how upsetting this must all be for Mary.

Luckily, Mary knew about radiation sickness. If the dose had been substantial there likely would be sickness for twenty-four days with the effects thereafter more hidden . . . like time bombs. A headache was to be expected if it was over 100 rem. As were the nausea and possibly, if she had more than a 200-rem dose, hair loss. Not having hair loss would signal she would survive and possibly have few aftereffects. Also, she had no headache or real nausea. She would use those signs as indicators of the severity of the radiation dose she had received. It had only been on her arm. And she had cleansed it immediately. Her arm did not appear to be burned. Dirty bombs she knew did not release radioactive iodine and she was too far from the plant for the water to be contaminated so no need for Potassium iodide (KI). Further, she knew that for a Dirty Bomb, treatment depended on the radioactive isotope. For example, for Cesium-137 (radioactive Cesium) the drug of choice is Prussian Blue, not KI. She only had KI, so she nixed that as possible precaution. If anything, she felt like she had a light case of the flu. Her temperature was above normal and occasionally she had a chill. She had a dry cough and was just inordinately tired. Perhaps she was only tired out by the intensity of the event and the worry. Just maybe she would luck out. She had her fingers crossed.

Lenore came into the room around dinner time. She brought with her a tray of food.

“Mary, can you sit up?”

Mary tried but was unsuccessful.

Lenore placed the tray on the top of the bureau and pulled Mary up to a sitting position after which Mary leaned against her arm as Lenore placed two pillows behind her back and moved Mary closer to them so she could lean against them.

"There," said Lenore. "How's that." Mary leaned against the pillows. "Better."

Lenore pushed back Mary's hair and arranged Mary's blankets after which she brought over the tray which had legs that opened down to form a table over Mary's legs. "Chicken soup, tomato juice, milk, and bread pudding. Look good?"

Mary responded with a weak smile but just sat there. "I wonder where my boys are. I'm sure they are safe. Jason would know what to do. Still, I wonder."

Lenore pulled a chair that was near the bed closer, picked up the spoon and began to feed Mary. As she did so, she occasionally made a comment or posed a question. "I'm sure the boys are safe. And you are right about Jason knowing what to do."

"I hope so."

Lenore thought to help to take her mind from the boys. "So, Mary, where have you been these last several days?"

"Home."

Lenore fed Mary more soup and thought on that. Had Lou been closer? Too close? Had he survived? Was he in a hospital unconscious? Or was it just that without the telephone lines he had not called . . . maybe walled up in an extreme situation?

"Yes. With the phones out, it's hard to know what happened. But what is there to do?"

"Exactly."

"So where do you think the boys headed, Mary?" "I don't know."

Lenore was incredulous but she kept her face neutral. "What do you know?"

“Only what they said in a note Jason left.”

“Yes?”

“Rather than hunker down they had left. They were ‘going north.’” “Why would they do that?”

“Well, we had talked about what to do if the Plant went down.”

“Yes.”

“And how if we heard about it within the first half hour we could leave before any fallout might arrive. They must have heard about it immediately.”

“Or maybe they saw the fires.”

“Fires?”

“Yes. And Carlos told me that fires were visible almost immediately. He arrived before us.”

“Oh. That explains it.”

“Carlos thought it might be arson. Or maybe dirty bombs.”

“Yes. They probably saw them and, on the chance the Plant had gone down, left quickly and hitched a ride.”

“Yes. Probably.”

“But Jason is resourceful. And Marty idolizes him and probably followed his lead.”

“Yes.”

“Their bikes were gone. And the money stashed for any ‘in case’. And the backpacks . . . but you all stayed?”

“Yes. We just hunkered down for three days . . . still are. Same thought. Just in case the Plant had gone down. Is that what you did?"

"Yes. I stayed in our basement hideaway room.

"We did the same. Used the downstairs center hall and a chamber pot."

"I wonder what others did?"

"I don't know. Haven't seen anyone to ask.'

Lenore knew that the key terms in surviving radiation sickness care were cleanliness and hydration. She knew that if infection evidenced, they might also use antibiotics, but the hospitals would be overrun. If Mary brought up the idea of being checked out in the hospital, Lenore would tell her that and advise she stay and rest and she would keep her clean and hydrated and that it would be better to wait and watch.

When Mary finished her meal, she lay back in the pillows.

"Okay, Mary. Rest. But don't lie down for forty-five minutes." Lenore gave her a jaunty look. "You don't want GERD."

Mary smiled. "No, I don't want GERD."

As Lenore rose to take the tray away, Mary followed her with her eyes. "Everyone should have as caring friends as you and your family . . . and as informed."

A bit later, Lenore returned carrying a basin of water, a towel, a washcloth, and soap. "Wash up time!" she chimed. With her was Ricky with a plastic place mat which he put on the night table beside the bed and upon which Lenore placed the basin.

"Hi, Mary. How are you?" asked Ricky. Stephen had followed them in and stood at the bottom of the bed.

"Oh. A little tired. But I'll be fine."

"You got radiafon on you, Mary?" It was Stephen.

"Yes. But I cleaned it off quickly and showered when I got home so I'll be okay. Not to worry, Stephen."

"Where's Marty?"

"Oh, went north. With Jason."

"Why?"

"Well, they wanted to be sure they would be safe."

"They shudda' come here."

"Well, I guess they didn't want to bother you. And they just were going for a few days."

"When are they coming back?"

"After we talk to them and I am ready for them to come home."

"Oh." Ricky turned on his heel and headed out of the room. "I miss them," he said as he left.

"Anything else, Mom?" asked Ricky. "No. We're fine," said Lenore.

After Ricky left, Lenore closed the door and helped Mary disrobe after which, she covered her, washed her face and arms and hands, and followed them by washing a quarter of Mary's body at a time. Then leaving Mary to lie under the blankets, Lenore left for a few minutes and returned with a clean nightgown.

"So, Mary, I think I should be here whenever you get up to go to the bathroom."

"I think so, too. I managed before lunch, but I need to go again now, and I do feel weak."

So together they made their way to the bathroom adjacent to the room and Lenore waited until Mary was ready and accompanied her back to the bed. Lenore made sure she was comfortable in the bed and Mary said, "I think I'll take a nap now."

"You do that, Mary. Just call if you need anything and one of us will come."

"Thank you, Lenore. Thank you so much."

Mary knew that as the sickness progressed, her natural defenses against infection would wain and her vulnerability to illness increase. She also knew that hydration was essential to washing away the waste and any germs or viruses that might accumulate within her. She spoke to Lenore about her needs, but as she had already demonstrated, Lenore already understood as one had to when one lived so close to a nuclear power plant: One did the research.

They would all wait it out together.

Carlos and the boys and Lenore were wonderful. The boys' school was closed, and Carlos did not go to work and was careful to conserve on gas as the gas stations did not all have generators and the lines were long at those that did. Luckily, he was a reader, so he read much of the time. Or played games with the boys. Or just sat and talked.

Lenore kept busy with her household duties and Carlos did the shopping, generally taking the boys with him and shopping in places north of them and hence further from the Plant. North of them there was electricity and gas stations were functioning normally, so it was easier to keep the tank full.

As the days passed, Mary's exhaustion remained her main symptom. Her temperature ran around 100 degrees Fahrenheit and occasionally she felt chilled. The cough lingered but did not become worse. Her hair stayed rooted. And despite for a general achiness, she really did not have a headache. Lenore let her sleep, waking her for sustenance and water and to be washed or to have her bed linens changed and by the end of the second week, Mary began to feel well enough to sit up and dangle her legs onto the floor. She even took some solid food and held her own glass of juice. She pulled on her hair. It remained firmly rooted. Gradually she was concluding the dose she had received was 100 rem or less and that with time she would be fine with little likelihood of after-effects. Mary's sense of time was not at its best. It had been seventeen days since the event. The phones and electricity were up, and her plan was to begin to search for Lou and the boys. She thought she'd start with the Red Cross. She just didn't feel quite up to it yet. But her decision was to start on the coming Monday, May 6, 2018.

TWO Jason and Marty

April 12, 2018

Jason carried the terrarium to the edge of the stream. Marty tagged along to watch and to say whatever goodbyes there were to be said as Rocky slithered away. Jason removed the top screen and angled the terrarium to suggest a direction for Rocky to take. The snake raised its head higher, hesitated but a moment, and then sped off across the rocks and down a crevice without even so much as a backward glance. Marty wanted to check out the size of the tadpoles in the stream, so Jason joined him for a bit. Then Jason returned to the terrarium, stood the screen at an angle within it, and grabbed it by one of its glass sides for transport. Together he and Marty headed back for the house.

Once inside, Jason poured himself a cold glass of milk and Marty ran himself a drink of water from the tap, then buttered a slice of whole wheat bread with some peanut butter and jelly, slapped a second slice on top of it and cut it crosswise, giving half to Jason.

“Thanks.”

The boys stood silently, eating, and drinking and looking at each other. They rinsed their glasses under the faucet, shoved them upside down in the dishwasher, and headed for the cellar, Jason in the lead. Marty had never really liked the dark, dry atmosphere of the cellar, but with his brother there ahead of him it seemed less spooky. Once down there, they headed for the bikes, which were stored inside the windowless center room once used for storing wood for the old fireplace in the living room. When their parents bought the house, his mom and dad had mentioned a number of times that the wood room would be a great room in case there ever was a need to “hunker down,” as his dad called it. At first Marty had thought his dad meant squatting with knees bent, but as time passed, he came to understand it was for use in case of certain emergencies. Like a hurricane, they had noted. Or in case of fallout. The explanation of the room’s importance left Marty more confused than ever. He had never heard of a hurricane happening around here. And if any of them were to have a fight and fall out, why any one of them would want to use a windowless room as a “time out” was beyond him.

Over the past winter, the boys’ mom and dad had some shelves built in the room on which they stored all kinds of first aid supplies, canned foods, bottles of water, a bucket with a box of plastic bags in it, sweat pants and sweatshirts for each of them, along with flip-flops and dad’s dosimeter. His dad said they always needed them at work to measure the radiation levels. Marty figured his dad didn’t take this one to work because they gave him one to use free when he was there, which probably saved on batteries. He knew, too, that Jason understood how it worked because he had gotten up to go to the bathroom one night and his dad was explaining it to Jason at the kitchen table. There also was a box of what his dad said was KI. Marty had opened it. What was in it looked like a batch of white pills resembling aspirin. He decided that when and if they ever got around to having the fight, which would really have to be a big one— although over what he could not guess—that they would probably all need to take aspirin and that was why the batch was so big.

Before the boys could leave for their bike ride, Jason had to tighten his chain, and as both bikes had sat over the winter, the chains were dusty and needed greasing. The boys pulled their bikes out into the middle of the north side of the cellar where dad kept his tools on a work bench. The bench stood against the north wall of the wood room, as everyone in the family referred to the room to be used in case of emergencies as a shelter and in case of major differences or, as the younger boy believed, as a time out. Why it remained the wood room when its use no longer had anything to do with fuel was something of a mystery to Marty.

Marty wandered about, waiting for instruction from Jason. He perused the wood room.

He was convinced that grownups were a special bunch, always throwing in one word or another to get you mixed up. *They should have called it the storeroom. Look at this. Four sleeping bags, no less. Never even taken out of their cases.* He bounced one that was still in its plastic case against the wall. He picked up the box of travel games that no one was allowed to remove from the room. Last spring, he had wanted to take it to Chicago when they drove there for Easter. NO WAY! *He never could figure out what that was all about!*

Dad once said that the wood room could well be considered the most important room in the house.

Figure that. Dad. What a joker.

It took quite a while to decide which would be the best tools to use for removing and replacing the chains. To not leave his younger brother out of the process, as Jason searched, he talked about what he was doing.

"Let's see, now. A-1. No." Jason replaced the flattened can with the pointed nose back on the shelf.

He should have asked his dad which oil or grease to use. "What are you doing in there? Come on, Marty. Help."

Marty exited the wood room and joined Jason in front of his dad's worktable Jason inspected the cans on the shelf, pulling them out one at a time, and then quickly replacing them. "*Wasps and bees*. No. *Good on Wood*. Nope. *Axle grease*. Yup. *Pay dirt*." He opened a tightly closed tin can in which grease that looked like dark Vaseline was to be found. He held it down for Marty to inspect. He stuck his finger in it, held it to his nose, smelled it. "Yup. Axle grease."

He swiped it beneath Marty's nose and Marty followed suit. "Yup. Axle grease."

"Now, where did dad put those plastic gloves?" "Here they are!"

Suddenly, the floor shook beneath them. The cans on the shelf rattled as did the tools. Some fell to the floor. The lights went out. The boys froze. Stock-still in the dim light of the cellar, they sought each other's eyes.

"Stay with me. Come on." Jason led the way up the stairs and Marty followed closely behind. Jason went to the south side living room window. Marty crowded in beside him to get a look, too. What the boys saw was pretty incredible. The whole southern sky was glowing like red hot coals. Jason was unable to estimate how far away the glow was but giving a good guess, if it were the Magdum Heights Plant, it was thirty miles south or so. And if it were not, then it was just a large fire only a few miles from where they stood.

In either case, they were not particularly well situated. Jason's thought went to his mother and father. What went through his mind filled him with dread and a sickening, sinking feeling. His brother brought him back.

"Jason. Holy Moley!"

The traffic light on the old secondary road that led north to the thruway was still working. Quite possibly those traveling it were still unaware of the disaster. The trees might have hidden the fires from drivers' views. Also, those coming south may have been too far north to have seen the fire's first flare. Jason still wasn't sure if what looked like an enormous conflagration indicated a meltdown or was just a big fire, but they weren't hanging around to find out.

Given the thorough preparations his mom had provided for him, Jason was quite sure they had left the house within five minutes and definitely in less than ten of seeing the blaze—or whatever it was. Beyond the fact they were hitching, all looked as usual.

Jason maintained a pace just fast enough to permit Marty to stay beside him without having become winded. Within eight or nine minutes they were at the thruway. He figured if they could get a ride in the next five minutes, in thirty-five minutes they might be some twenty-five minutes north of Ariana or about fifty miles from Magdum Heights. He doubted that on such a windless day any fall-out would reach that far north so quickly—unless the force of the explosion had propelled it—but he had never heard that factored in at such a distance and he had not seen a plume. If he could just keep them moving north, his plan was to grab a lift on the thru-way north, travel seventy-five miles and be one hundred miles from The Plant within an hour or two. So soon after an event, one hundred miles would be home free—if they could just reach Bain before dinner hour, if someone would just stop.

The traffic on the highway was still light and as soon as there was a break, they crossed its four lanes to the east side, ditched their bikes, and started walking north. Each time a car approached, Jason raised his thumb. After a bit, an old man in a truck with homemade wooden sides on it stopped. The driver called out to them through the half open window.

"Whatchu' boys upta, now? Why ain'tcha in school?"

"Parent-teacher conference day. We need to get to Waxton." Jason guessed that the truck had no air conditioning. It was also possible it had no radio.

"Yeah," chimed in Marty. "We have to meet our grandparents

there."

"They tell you to hitchhike?'

"Yeah." Marty again. "My dad's truck broke down near 'em."

Boy, Marty was good! Jason picked up the beat. Indicating his bag, he said, "Yeah, I have to bring him some spark plugs and jumper cables."

"Yeah." Marty again.

"Okay, hop in. I don't usually do this, but I don't like to see kids out on the road. Got grandkids uv m'own, ya' know."

In the effort to separate the man from Marty, Jason climbed in first, just in case. He lodged his backpack on the floor beside his feet. Beneath him, the seat bumped up somewhat uncomfortably. He stretched his feet to the right of the bump in the floor above the transmission. This left little remaining room for Marty's feet and backpack, but anything that would get them closer to Bain was fine with him.

Marty settled in beside his brother, his backpack beside Jason's and his feet squidged tight against the seat. The truck door needed oiling, but with a second pull from Jason, it closed, and the truck veered onto the road.

Jason sighed. They were on their way.

* * *

“Well, this is as far as I go.” The old man pulled over into a gas station not far after the road sign read Bixby. “My home is down this next street. You can come there and use my phone to reach your dad. Or you can use the pay phone here.”

“Thanks, Hank. I’ll use this one. Come on, Marty. Open the door.”

Marty pulled down the handle and swung the door open. “Thanks a lot for the lift, Hank.”

“You’re welcome, Marty.”

“Yeah. Thanks so much, Hank,” said Jason, offering his hand to the aged man.

“Well, you know where I am if you need me. Number 10. Down that street.”

“Thanks.” Jason descended from the truck and slammed the door with the force he had learned was what it took to do it right.

“See ya,” said Hank, putting the old clunker in gear and taking off.
“See ya,” said the boys in unison.

THREE Lou Matters

April 12 to August 23, 2018

It was late morning when Lou left Magdum Heights Plant and headed for the parking area. His car keys and cell phone in the ready, he pulled out his wallet to replace his Plant ID card. As he did, a blast from seemingly nowhere hit him and lifted and threw him against the rock ledge that dropped down to the right of the parking lot entrance. When he woke, he was in a hospital bed in Aesopolis where he had been in a coma at least a day. A nurse entered. He wanted to ask her something, but no words formed. He watched her as she checked the drip bag. Looking down she seemed startled to find him looking at her.

"Hello," she said. "Are you awake?"

Lou blinked his eyes in response.

"Can you talk?"

Lou blinked again.

She patted his arm. "I'll be right back," she said.

On her return she brought an older man and a young woman. Lou, read their badges. "Martin George, MD, Neurologist; Connie LaSalle, SLP, Speech-Language Pathologist."

Dr. George offered his hand to Lou. "I'm Martin George, your doctor. You've had a pretty severe injury to the head."

"I'm Connie Williams. I'm a speech language pathologist." Connie had with her a card with picsyms and writing on it. "Is speaking difficult for you?"

Lou blinked twice quickly.

"Yes. I thought so. So, for now we will use yes/no questions. You can answer with one blink for yes and two for no. Do you understand me?"

Lou blinked once.

"Good. Can you read this card?"

Lou blinked once.

"Do you know your name?"

Lou searched his memory. Lou. Yes, that was it. Lou.

Lou blinked once.

"Can you point to the letters that spell it?"

Lou pointed with his right hand. L-O-U.

"Lou?" asked the nurse.

Lou blinked once.

"Do you know your last name?"

Lou searched his memory. Clatters? Mitters? He was not sure. He blinked twice.

"That's okay, Lou. You've just wakened. You've been sleeping a long time. We'll let you rest. Think of me as Connie and this is Dr. George. You are doing well. We'll see you later."

* * *

Connie and Dr. George were in a conference area. "What do you think, Doctor?"

"Given the extent of the damage to the right side of his brain and the lesser to the left side, the fact he remembered his first name is encouraging."

"And he could spell it."

"Yes, and even more so is the fact that he can read which further suggests his language functions may be supported receptively through reading."

"He's still a pretty disabled pup." Connie thought a minute. "His coma lasted at least a day.'

"Yup. And any post traumatic amnesia is pretty likely to last weeks to months."

"Hopefully, he will recall his last name . . . it would sure be nice if he had some family around at this time."

"The good thing about his coma is that at least much of the pain from the bruising he suffered to his side and hip should be hurting less than it would have right after the event."

"I suppose."

The doctor was typing into a laptop. "And his being awake lessens the need for passive physical therapy and brings in the need for active."

"He'll probably suffer weakness."

"Yes." He was still inputting info into the computer. "And the likelihood of his exhibiting left side neglect is strong . . . He pointed with his right hand. With luck he is also right-handed."

"So, you think there will be left-side neglect?"

The doctor nodded.

"When I work with him, I'll take care to sit in front of him or to his right . . . And I'll watch for signs of neglect in my assessment and treatment sessions."

"Yes. You'll need to evaluate him and in addition to active physical therapy, we'll set him up for daily feeding and speech language therapy. You can start today. The PT we'll start tomorrow."

When Connie returned to Lou's bedside, she cranked his bed up so he was at a sixty-degree angle. Using the one blink, yes; two blinks no system, she asked if he was comfortable. He was.

Connie had with her some custard in a plastic cup which she opened by pulling back the tinfoil cover.

"We need to find out if you can eat. Would you like to taste this?" Lou blinked.

When Connie gave Lou a quarter of a teaspoon of the custard, he opened his mouth then closed his lips around it and after a bit swallowed. The food went down without a difficulty. Slowly he managed the whole quarter cup.

“That was great!”

Lou gave a weak smile.

“For now, we will start you on pureed food. We’ll try some soft foods tomorrow.”

Lou looked up at the intravenous

“That will have to stay until you are eating meals. But not to worry. You are doing well.”

Lou blinked once.

Connie pulled out a pad and pencil. “Can you write the ABCs”

Lou’s writing was large and loose and took up the right side of the paper . . . a . . . d . . . L . . .b

“Thank you, Lou.” Well, he could write. Sequence was absent and content was incomplete. And . . . Connie observed he had written only on the right half of the paper. Yes . . . left side neglect.

Next Connie showed Lou a chart with picsyms on it. Written under the icons were the words *drink, eat,* TV, *turn over, sit up, lie down, and pain, and* Yes/No.

Connie pointed to pain. “Do you have any pain, Lou?”

Lou shook his head no. Connie pointed to NO. Lou shook his head yes. Connie would remove the Yes/No for tomorrow and perhaps add bathroom. In that way, the nurses would not have to be so careful about asking Lou if he had to use the bathroom.

“Can you point to the cup?”

Lou pointed to the cup.

Connie said and mimed, "Drink."

"What did you do with the custard, Lou?"

Lou pointed to eat.

"That's a lot, Lou. I will let you rest."

Lou put out his hand toward the card and Connie showed it again.

Lou pointed to, "Lie down."

Connie readjusted his bed to a thirty-degree angle and Lou was asleep before she left the room.

* * *

It had been two weeks since Lou had returned from the coma. Physical therapy occurred three times a day. He was lifting his arms and legs on his own in a prone position and was able to sit with his legs over the side of the bed for five or so minutes before extreme fatigue overcame him and he had to lie down. He had left side weakness but could move his limbs. He needed prompts to use his left hand. His food continued to be given to him in custard or pureed form, but he was eating a little three times a day, sitting erect in bed as he did so, and for the most part, if things were arranged toward his right side, feeding himself. His ribs hurt him but apparently, they were just bruised and would heal and the bruise on his hip continued to fade. His mood varied and sometimes for no reason he would become quite angry.

On that day when Connie came in to feed him, he knocked the custard from her hand and stared at her menacingly.

"It's okay, Lou. You are all right."

Lou looked embarrassed.

"It's the injury. Sometimes it makes you angry."

Lou looked at Connie intensely. "Talk," he said.

"Oh, Lou. You said talk! You spoke!"

"Talk," said Lou. "Talk."

Mary took out a pad from her pocket. On it she wrote, "Talk." She showed it to Lou.

"Talk," read Lou.

Connie wrote, "Lou talk." "Lou talk," read Lou.

Connie added her name.

"Lou talk Connie," read Lou and fell back on his pillows, too tired to do more.

Connie rolled his bed down to thirty degrees and left him sleeping. Lou was talking!

Connie had made a number of flashcards. They read:

I'm Lou.

Hello, Connie.

Hi, Dr. George.

Want water.

Want eat.

Weather?

Day?

Lou could read them all aloud. His sounds were a bit sloppy, but he was understandable. One day when Connie entered his room he said, "Hello, Connie."

Lou progressed in spurts and starts. Some days he could find words without the need for written words. Other days even the written words were difficult and tiring. But one way or another, he was very gradually building physical strength and spoken vocabulary. He still evidenced periods of sudden but short-lived anger accompanied by a sense of embarrassment thereafter. But he continued to never mention his family or the past. He seemed to live only in the present. Connie hoped the television soaps would boost his recall, but he could not attend to them for more than a few minutes and mostly preferred no television. So, Connie brought in some magazines. Sports Illustrated. People. At first, she just left them on his tray. He showed no interest in them. So, Connie brought in some picture cards she had of children, adults, and families doing things usual to family life and in each session, she would show Lou a few of the cards and make simple statements about their content. "The mother is feeding the baby." "The little girl is swinging." "The children are playing."

One day Connie brought in a picture of two middle school aged boys looking at a frog.

"I have boys," said Lou.

"Oh, you do?" said Mary. She waited a bit. "Do they go to school?"

"Yes."

"Do they play sports?"

"Catch frogs. Ride bikes," answered Lou.

"Oh, your boys . . . your sons . . . catch frogs? Ride bikes?"

"Yes. Jason."

"Jason rides a bike?"

"Yes. And Marty."

"Oh, both Jason and Marty ride bikes."

"What about their mom?"

"Drives a car."

"You drive?" asked Lou.

"Yes. I drive to work."

Lou changed the topic. "Eat soon?"

"Yes, we eat soon."

And so, Connie learned that Lou had two sons, Jason and Marty, and a wife. But she knew she had to be careful. There was no way to force memory. And she did not want to anger Lou.

Maybe, though, if he recalled his wife's name, he would also recall his family name. Maybe tomorrow.

* * *

As the weeks passed, Lou was increasingly awake and verbal and had begun to walk independently for short periods. On that day, Connie was providing therapy for Lou in a small sunroom off the main hall. A storm was brewing outside.

Lou viewed the coming storm. "Hope Jason and Marty are home from school."

"They probably are," Connie reassured him.

"Mary comes home later than they do."

"Oh?"

"But Jason will watch over Marty."

"Yes," responded Connie and waited a bit. "What does Mary do?"

"Same."

"Same?"

"Same."

"Same as you?"

"Same as you."

"Mary helps people talk?"

"Yes."

"Do I know her?"

"Do you know her?"

Connie decided to risk it. "What's her name?"

"Mary Matters." Connie decided to push further. "Oh. And you're Lou Matters?" "Lou and Mary Matters."

Rather than calling attention to the enormous step Lou had made in his recall, Connie simply said, "I bet you are both really proud of Jason and Marty."

Lou smiled and gave her a nod and they headed back to his room so he could rest, and Connie was able to leave and bring the good news to Dr. George. Lou Matters . . . Lou's family name was Matters.

It was August 23, 2018. Five months since Lou's injury.

FOUR In the Woods

April 12 –October 17, 2018

Jason would remember what Hank had said . . . Number 10 . . . down that street.

And there they were . . . some forty five miles from home, Jason with a wad of fifteen hundred dollars in bills in his pocket . . . the money his father had put in the go-to room in case of emergencies . . . and Marty, looking to his brother for direction.

Jason looked around. "Well, my man, we're out. We're safe. We just need a plan."

Off to the left behind the gas station was a stretch of wooded area. Jason needed time to think.

"Let's see if we can get some food in here, Marty."

They entered the gas station. There was a see-through glass

refrigerator on one of its counters.

Packaged sandwiches lined its lower shelf. Jason opened the door. "Take a couple, Marty."

Marty grabbed a tuna and a turkey. Jason took a turkey and a ham.

On the counter were some high protein bars. Jason picked up six. Then the two of them headed for the drinks fridge. Two bottles of chocolate milk. Two of pop. That would do it. They paid at the counter and split their purchases between their two backpacks, used the men's room, and left.

Outside Jason headed around the back of the station. Marty traipsed on after him. Together they entered the shade of the woods. Walking inward until they could no longer see the road, Jason suggested they sit.

"Time to chow down."

The two boys ate in silence and drank a pop. "Okay, Marty. Ever onward."

They rose and walked another few minutes deeper into the woods where they came upon a ramshackle small abandoned house. It was paintless, but its windows and door were intact. The porch was rotted and missing some boards. Jason treaded gingerly across its surface. It held. He tried the door. It swung open with a creak. They entered.

The floor plan was simple. Two bedrooms and a living area with wood stove. No sink. No toilet. But dry. Probably more than a hundred years old. Maybe an original settler of Bixby.

"Here we are, Marty." Jason placed his backpack on one of the beds. Marty placed his on the one on the opposite wall. Luck. And close enough to walk to the gas station for food and phoning.

A walk outside revealed an outhouse and a water pump. Jason gave the pump handle some pumps. Nothing. It needed priming. Jason recalled priming one on his aunt's farm when they visited her last summer.

Not far from the house was a stream. "Marty, bring out the kettle from the stove. We need it to get water from the stream."

The water streamed from the kettle into the pump water passage tube. Jason pumped. Marty brought more water. Jason pumped. More water. Et voila! Water streamed from the pump.

Jason filled the kettle and took it into the house. They could use it for washing but they would purchase their drinking water at the gas station. A search of the house was easy. Everything was either in the open or in one of the cabinets against the walls between the beds in each bedroom. Jason found sheets. They were pretty much dust free. He threw Marty two and took two for himself. Together the boys turned over the mattresses and put the sheets on the beds. In the closet in the other room they found two blankets. They spread them on their respective beds. There was a broom in the kitchen. They would use that later. But for now, Jason was tuckered out. He kicked off his shoes and climbed into bed. Marty followed suit and before long, they were both sleeping.

For dinner they ate the other sandwiches and drank the chocolate milk. Jason thought he would go to the station and try calling home. And they could pick up something for morning. Doubtful their situation would change much before then.

At the gas station they bought more sandwiches, some Danish, bottled water, and more chocolate milk. They also bought two flashlights and a double supply of batteries. And a padlock.

Together the two boys trudged on back to the cabin. That was in April.

* * *

Initially Jason went every day to the gas station, but the phone was not working at their home. Then after a week, although it did not take messages, it began to ring. But no one picked up. As for his mom's cell, Jason found it was dead. As was his dad's. He tried early morning, afternoon, and night. No one was home and no one could tell him where his parents were. Or how they were. And going back was out of the question as the news was so unclear, he could not tell if the area were safe. After a couple of weeks of ringing and no answer on the home phone, on May 3, he gave up. Here they had shelter, food, and water.

He had tried a couple of times since then with no better luck. Then he stopped trying.

It was like he and Marty were on a roughing it vacation.

Jason spent nothing on other than food, soap, and essentials. And the man in the gas station had him help lunch times and paid him cash under the table. So, Jason was able to hang on to his . . . their . . . cash.

* * *

Night was the most difficult.

It was dark in the room. Jason thought he heard Marty sob. Marty's voice wafted across to Jason. "Jason."

"What's up, Marty?"

"Do you ever wonder about Mom and Dad?"

"Yeah. All the time. Unless I'm busy doing something." "Do you think they could still be alive?"

"Oh. I think so. Mom would have been at or coming from work. Dad would have been going to lunch. They were supposed to meet and eat together. What with Mom having a half day."

"Then why haven't we news of them?"

"Well, with the meltdown, all the communications systems went down, too."

"So, what happened when you called?"

"The line was dead." Jason decided he would not tell Marty that when it did begin to ring, the answering machine was not on and still no one answered.

"How long does it take to fix it."

"You mean the electronic grid?"

"Yeah. I guess."

"Long time. But not to worry. We're safe and I am sure they are,

too."

"But what if they are not?"

"Problem is, there's not much we can do about it. So, the best thing to do is to take care of ourselves and then when we hook up together again, they will not have to worry about us. In case they do have their own problems."

"Like what?"

"Radiation sickness. Injury. I think they are both recuperating in the hospital and that's why they are not home."

"How will we find them?"

"We have to wait. Maybe we hole up here for a while and then we go to Bain. By then, maybe the grid will be up and the Red Cross can help us."

"Good plan."

"Go to sleep. Tomorrow is another day."

In the corner of the cabin kitchen area, Jason had found an old fishing pole with a reel on it. He cleaned it up and bought some line and a couple of lures at a small odds-and-ends store they had found in the nearby village. Threading it in he knew how to do. His father had taught him.

"Let's see, Marty. I think I can do this."

"First you thread it through here then you tie a double knot to hold it on the reel. Let's see. Yeah, I remember. Dad said to wind it clockwise." He had threaded the line through the eyes on the rod down toward the reel and now he held it at an angle between his knees. He held the line between his fingers as he reeled it in.

"Just not to the top." He indicated the top of the line on the reel. "See Marty, you need a space here. See . . . between the top of the reel and the line.

"Done."

The two of them headed toward the stream where they had seen trout swimming. Marty had found a frying pan in the side compartment of the wood stove. Whatever they caught they would eat. There were potatoes to boil and carrots to go with it. Without a refrigerator or ice box, fish would provide the answer to their need for protein. Along with the eggs they'd bought.

The boys took turns casting. Gradually their casts became more competent. Marty got one way out in the middle of the stream and whammee! The line tugged downward! Reeling that baby in was a struggle but he did it! It must have been nearly twenty inches long!

Once in, they examined it. It had the dark spot at the bottom of its first dorsal fin and large teeth. Jason was sure that was what they called a walleyed perch. But no matter. Whatever its name, it would sure make a nice meal.

“Whoa, Marty. You did it! What a beauty! And just in time for dinner.”

* * *

The summer passed peacefully. Jason and Marty wandered together. Early mornings they would fish. Late mornings, Marty hung around at the station while Jason worked. Afternoons they wandered in the woods and a couple of afternoons a week they wandered into the small village area nearby. Jason picked up some books to read, and Marty followed suit. Also, they bought some cards. They played Slap Jack, Solitaire, and Four Kings in Corners. Jason won two out of three games, but Marty offered good competition.

Occasionally they would speculate about their parents. Or share stories of things they had done. Sometimes Marty would tear up in their discussions. But not Jason. He remained stoically in control. Not that he didn’t wonder. But keeping Marty safe and the two of them going along was his main concern. They would search for their parents in the fall.

FIVE Left Side Neglect

End of May 2018 - August 23, 2018

By the end of May, Mary had returned to her home. She still needed a nap in the day but overall, she was feeling well . . . except for the way the days dragged onward without word from the boys or Lou.

Every day she opened the Red Cross Safe and Well and the National Website for Missing Persons at www.namus.gov websites and entered Lou and the boys' names in the search engine. She tried Lou as Lewis and Louis with and without his middle named. She did the same with Jason and Marty entering Jay and Martin and with and without their middle names. Nothing.

Once a week she called her sister in Ohio . . . just to be in touch. Her parents and Lou's were all deceased and so except for her sister, she had no family other to contact.

It was late August 2018. At 4:30 in the afternoon the telephone rang. Mary jumped to get it. Since the Event, she received few phone calls. The boys' friends knew they were not there. And of course, neither they nor their father called.

"Hello?"

"Hello. I'm looking for a Mary Matters?" "I'm she."

"Yes. Well, Mrs. Matters, I'm calling from the American Red

Cross."

"Yes?"

"We have located one Lou Matters. Not to worry. He is fine. Do you know him?"

"I do."

"How do you know him?"

"I'm his wife. The mother of his children."

"Excellent."

"What can you tell me about him?"

"Well he is currently at the Waxton Rehabilitation Center perhaps twenty miles north of Ariana. Have you heard of it?"

"Yes. I'm a speech language pathologist and know where it is. How is he?"

"He is doing well and would like to see you. Can you come?" "I'll be there in a half an hour."

Mary hung up the phone, reached for her purse and keys, and headed out of the house. As she left, she rang Lenore.

"Lenore. Can you believe it? I am on my way to see Lou. He is at the Waxton Rehabilitation Center and asking for me."

At Waxton, Mary asked at the front desk for Lou and a young woman came out to greet her.

"Hello, Mrs. Matters. I'm Connie LaSalle. I do speech language therapy with your husband. It's a pleasure. And he is doing very well."

"Pleased to meet you. Can I see him?"

Connie led Mary down the hall to an end room with a table and some chairs in it. Lou was sitting at the table. He rose when she entered and held out his right hand to her. His smiled assured her he was glad to see her.

"Hello, Lou."

"Hello, Mary."

"How are you?" "I'm doing well."

Mary noted that his speech was clear, his hand grasp firm. She sat herself in the first seat nearest him . . . on his left side.

Connie interrupted. "Excuse me, Mrs. Matters. For now, it would be better if you sat on Lou's right side. He has difficulty seeing things on his left. When we are involved in helping lessen that, I will ask you to sit on his left. But for now, I think you just want to see one another."

Left side neglect were the first words that came to Mary's mind. "Thank you, Connie . . . may I call you Connie?" Connie said she preferred that and sat herself facing Lou. Mary changed sides of the table.

"So, Lou. It's been so long. I have missed you terribly."

"And I have missed you, Mary. And the boys."

"Yes. Of course. The boys." Mary directed her gaze at Connie. "Can you tell me how Lou's been doing? How long he has been here?"

"Yes. Well he arrived from the hospital here at the Rehabilitation Center early in May. He had suffered right side injuries . . . fractured ribs, bruised hip, and right-side brain injury. He had been in a coma for more than a day. He was transported here shortly thereafter. About eight or nine weeks ago now."

"Does he receive both PT and ST?"

"Yes. You are familiar with our rehab program?"

"Only how rehabs work. You see I, too, am a speech language pathologist."

"Oh, lovely, Mrs. Matters!"

"Please call me Mary."

"Mary."

Lou seemed happy just sitting beside Mary. He held her hand and Connie and Mary talked. Connie mentioned that the PT was helpful with the left side weakness . . . paresis . . . Lou exhibited in his left arm and hand. She said he was making good progress with it but still needed prompts to use his left arm and hand in dressing and eating.

She also said he was receiving OT to encourage the use of his left hand for cutting food, dressing, buttoning his shirt, and holding a paper when writing,

Connie mentioned how in speech language therapy they were working on sequencing and comprehending metaphors and analogies and understanding jokes as well as writing more complex sentences. She mentioned how it was through reading aloud that his early starts in speech were made.

Mary inquired as to when they thought he might be able to go home.

“That depends. He needs someone with him as his judgement is not always the best.”

“Like when?”

“Well, he often thinks he can do things he is not ready to do. Particularly activities requiring his use of both hands and careful scanning. For that reason, we only allow him to use the stove with supervision. We’ve observed how he fails to note when pans on the left side of the stove need water or need to be turned down.”

“Oh. I can understand that.”

“Or he will attempt to pick up an item too heavy for him to carry without the use of his left arm. One day, for instance, he wanted to be helpful and take out the kitchen garbage, but he forgot his left arm is weak and when he tried to move the garbage, it tipped over onto the floor on his left.”

“That must have been embarrassing for you, Lou. I’m sorry.” Lou just smiled.

“No, he didn’t seem embarrassed. In fact, because he didn’t seem to see it, he went on with his activities without a second thought toward cleaning it up.”

“So perhaps it is too early to come home full time. Also, come September, I return to work.”

Connie nodded in agreement. “But perhaps I might bring him home to visit on some days.”

“Possibly.”

“What do you think, Lou? Would you like to come home to visit?" Lou smiled.

Mary noted Lou's general silence. He seemed to follow the conversation; however, where once he had been so easily verbal, now he said little.

SIX To Bixby

October 17, 2018

Fall colored the woods around the boys. They had settled into their rustic life. Today they were near the cabin ensconced in apple trees that had not been pruned or sprayed in a long time. The apples were a little ratty, but as the two of them sat on branches of adjacent trees, munching the good parts of the Macs was a pleasurable pastime.

“So, Marty. I’ve been thinking.”

“Yeah.”

“Yeah.

“Winter’s coming.”

“I spose.”

“We need better digs.”

“Yeah. I spose.”

“So, what I’ve been thinking is we move.”

“Move where?”

“I don’t know where yet. But I thought maybe we could hitch a ride into Bixby. There have to be other people still on the road who left to escape the meltdown.”

“Yeah. Bixby.” The name turned on a light in Marty’s head. The Red Cross. They could look for Mom and Dad.

“Well, they must have shelters for them.” “Ya think so?”

“Yeah.”

Marty was quiet a while. “Wonder if Hank has any plans of going to Bixby any time soon.”

“Marty, you’re a genius.”

“He said he lived in number 10.”

“Can’t be far.”

And that is how it happened. They climbed down from the trees, shoved as many apples as they could into their pockets and headed off to find Hank. As they headed down Hank’s street, Jason spied Hank’s clunker of a truck.

“You see what I see, Marty?

“Yeah, Jason. I see what you see . . . Hank’s truck.”

They knocked on the door and a man’s voice answered, “C’mon in.”

“Well, look at you two. All summer tanned and healthy. Whatcha’ up ta’?”

Marty spoke, “Well, Hank, we were fixin’ to get a lift to Bixby. Our dad is up there on an assignment and he'd have to take time off to come for us so we were wondering if you might not be going to Bixby in the next couple of days."

"Well, danged if I'm not. Gotta deliver some wood to a family who like a real fire in their fireplace in the winter. So, they're just storin' in now. Goin' up tomorrow. Early. Say around six. Like ta' beat the traffic."

Jason gave Marty a smile. "Great! See you at six tomorrow. Have a good night!"

"You, too. What was it? Jason? Marty?"

"Yeah, you got it, Hank. I'm Jason. He's Marty."

* * *

That night as the boys packed their stuff together, Marty decided to raise the question of their parents. "So, Jason. Do you think we will be able to contact the Red Cross in Bixby? You know. About Mom and Dad?

I'm still worried about them, and I'd like to know where they are."

Jason took satisfaction in the notion that Marty seemed sure their parents were alive. As for Jason, that was not the case, and so while Marty wanted to contact the Red Cross immediately upon arrival in Bixby, Jason thought it might be better to put it off a bit.

Jason recalled his mom and her infectious laughter and his dad with his ability to think of fun things for the family to do . . . not to mention his serious side. Jason remembered him teaching him about a meltdown, its affects, survival in case one occurred, and his notion that in the event there ever were to be one, each one had to take care of him or herself . . . until it all calmed down and they could hook up together again.

For Jason, it had not calmed down enough . . . unless he were to find that in Bixby everything was back to normal, in which case he would contact the Red Cross.

Hank took them right to the center of Bixby. “You can get a bus from here to almost any place you want to go. Or a cab. You call your dad?”

“Yeah. He said to call when we get here, and he’d pick us up. Wherever we were.”

“Okay. Have a nice visit.” And he was off.

There was a Dunkin’ Donuts just across from where they descended. The boys crossed the street and entered. Jason patted the two twenties he had in his shirt pocket. The rest of what was left of the fifteen hundred their father had hidden for emergencies in the downstairs shelter room was in the bottom of his backpack in a wallet. He had been careful in its use and there was still more than a thousand left.

“A coffee and an egg on a biscuit,” ordered Jason. “What are you having, Mart?”

“Aw a container of milk and an egg sandwich. With ketchup.”

Seated, they sat at the counter, opened their sandwiches, and ate in silence. A couple sat down beside them.

“Morning.”

“Morning.”

“You boys are up and out early.”

"I guess we are. Meeting our dad. Our uncle just dropped us off on the way to work." And there was Marty. Always ready with an answer. How'd he do it. Maybe it was part of his beepin' and bobbin' and role playing around the house that let him always have a ready answer.

"Yeah," said Jason. "Say, we heard there are a lot of homeless people here in Bixby. You know. Since the meltdown."

"Tell me about it," said the man. "Why see that old hotel over there? They turned that into a shelter. Welcome everybody. . . and there is a smaller one around the corner and down the street. Used to be a store with a corner counter in it."

"Yes," said the woman. "They put up dividers and homeless people can just go there, sign in, and no questions asked, sleep there and get free meals."

"Ya, don't say." Marty again.

Jason gave him a nudge with his foot.

SEVEN Shelter

Oct 17, 2018

Jason and Marty left the Dunkin' Donuts.

"I think we should try the smaller one first, Marty. Wadaya think?"
"Yeah. Okay."

They headed out, down the street and around the corner. And sure enough, there it was. "Welcome" was clearly written on a board above the door.

Inside they were greeted by an older man. "Can I help you, boys?"

Jason stepped up to the counter. "Yes. We need a place to put up for a few nights. We're from downstate. Near the meltdown. We were hanging out in the woods, but winter is coming so they told us you run a shelter here."

"Yup." He turned a book toward Jason and handed him a pen. Just sign in here. Then just look around and find a bed that is clean and made. As for your stuff, you can put it in the locker beside it, lock it, and pocket the key. Dinner is at five. There is a clock over the door where you came in. The bathroom is down the hall."

The boys found themselves beds beside one another. They pushed aside the blanket that hung from a rope between them so they could see one another. They locked their backpacks in the lockers beside the beds and headed out to explore the area.

EIGHT In Bixby

October 2018 – May 17, 2019

The disaster relief center provided them a place to sleep and eat. Days, they wandered the streets and hung around in the library or went down to the waterfront. Going to the stores was not a good idea as their money was dwindling. And Marty had gotten into petty pilfering. All they had to do to survive was to show up at mealtime at the center.

Toward the end of October, a social service worker showed up and Jason explained how no one answered at home and so they were living at the Center. The social worker thought they should enroll in school and managed to order their records from their home school and in the beginning of November they started in classes at one of the local elementary schools. Marty made friends quickly and they invited him to come home with them after school and Jason picked up some cash for them in exchange for sweeping and cleaning at a supermarket nearby. With the money he earned, Jason bought his brother and himself school supplies.

Jason had decided at a point that it was time enough. He stopped calling home. His parents were gone. Who knew why or how? He would look for a job. He needed to keep replenishing their money. But somehow his promise to Marty to call the Red Cross came to him. He considered the situation. There were still disaster relief stations here so many miles from the site of the meltdown, who knew what it was like back home and up to thirty or thirty-five miles from it? Also, in his heart of heart he was convinced his parents were really gone from the face of the earth. Why else would they not have found them? So given these considerations, unless Marty brought it up, he would not look for the Red Cross to search for them.

The thought of his parents gone sickened Jason. He remembered his dad teaching him how to start the lawn mower and check its oil . . . his mom . . . cooking baked chicken and helping her to make the gravy. Tears welled in his eyed. He shook his head. Ever onward, he thought to himself . . . ever onward.

Jason walked into the Cali's Market that was a few blocks from the center. He looked on the bulletin board. There were some 3 x 5 cards with requests for help on them. Two interested him. One read:

Dog Walker Needed Evenings
In Bixby City
Two adorable dogs
Telephone: 438-2610

The second read:

Person needed
to trim shrubbery and mow large lawn of older home

six blocks from downtown Bixby
Phone 438-8800

Jason used the phone in the pharmacy. He dialed first the dog walker person.

"Hello? Yes, I'm Jason Matters and I'm calling about the dog walking position."

"Oh. Yes. Have you done dog walking before?"

"No. But my brother and I love animals and they usually like us. We were interested in walking your dogs."

"Oh, two of you. Well just happens I have two miniature poodles. Roxie and Moxie. Brother and sister. And I need someone to give them their evening meal and to walk them around the neighborhood. And to pick up after them when they have finished their business. I don't get back from work until 8:00 and it's too late for them to be fed."

"Well, we'd love to do that."

"Do you live near here?"

"Yes, we do. My brother is going on eleven and, I am fourteen." Jason stated, "Well, almost."

"Yes. Well, it might work out. Can you come by this morning? I'm at home."

Jason got the man's name, address, and directions. The man lived in an apartment building on the second floor. He could just come up to apartment 212 when they arrived. He dialed the second number. A woman answered.

"Hello?"

The voice that answered was cultured and light. "Hello?"

"Oh, yes. My name is Jason Matters. My brother and I would like to mow your lawn and care for your shrubberies."

"Oh. Two of you? That sounds like a nice idea. My dad used to hire out when he was a young whippersnapper and mow lawns and do shrubbery. You sound young?"

"Well, I'm almost fourteen and my brother is going on eleven."

"Hmm. Well, yes. Why don't you stop by so I can meet you both and we can talk about your responsibilities?"

And so it was that Jason and Marty came to keep themselves occupied evenings feeding and walking Mr. Alex's dogs and on the Saturday mornings through the late fall, mowing and primping the property of Mrs. Alice Sunderland . . . each week adding cash to their stash. Mr. Alex paid them forty dollars a week and Mrs. Sunderland paid them thirty dollars to keep the lawn and twenty to keep the bushes.

Of the ninety dollars, they agreed to bank sixty and that each of them gets fifteen for this and that. The plan was to save up a thousand dollars and then to move north where the cost of living was less and they could maybe get a room with heat and electricity in it in a house someplace toward the mountains in exchange for working on a farm.

Mr. Alex was young and had a business developing websites. He told the boys he had a couple of young people working for him, but they were in college and could only come late afternoons and evenings and that by the time he closed up and grabbed something to eat and drove home, it was seven-thirty or eight o'clock. He explained to Jason how he and Marty were to mix the wet food into the dry food and to add a little water for the two poodles and to have them sit and wait while they did so and come when it was the food was ready. He gave Jason a key to his apartment.

Marty seemed to have a way about him that feisty Moxie responded to and Roxie, a sweet and affectionate soul, became Jason's favorite.

It was a Saturday in late October. The boys had been tending Mrs. Sunderland's property for a couple of weeks. And it did need tending. Mrs. Sunderland had been in rehab for a broken ankle and her grounds keeper had retired just prior to that and had not been replaced. So, the boys had found the gardens overgrown and the grass badly in need of mowing. They went to work on the grass first. Marty mowed while Jason edged it. Once that was done, the area did on first glance look cared for, but the weeds in the bush, bulb, and flower beds were thick and the second week they let the lawn go and worked on them.

"Oh, you boys do such nice work!"

"Thanks, Mrs. Sunderland. It's not been easy." There was Marty. Saying what needed to be said.

"Oh, I know it. And I do appreciate your hard work!

"Thanks, Mrs. Sunderland." It was Jason's turn.

"But it is ten o'clock. Time for cookies and milk, don't you think?" "Sounds good to me," the boys chimed.

Each Saturday Mrs. Sunderland placed two glasses of milk and a dish of cookies on the table on the porch and invited the boys up for them. They came willingly and enjoyed their time there. Mrs. Sunderland went in the house while they snacked and would return in about fifteen minutes to ask them if they had had enough and to take away the plates and glasses. They had learned that Mrs. Sunderland was a widow and that her daughter was married and lived in North Carolina and only came to see her on holidays . . . although she had been up to see her while she was in rehab. But her daughter had several children and could only stay a few days.

Mrs. Sunderland had asked the boys about their parents and they explained they both worked Saturdays, their mom at the college and their dad with an air conditioning crew. The boys never went in her house and she did not invite them. And each Saturday at noon, she paid them in cash.

Mrs. Sunderland had gone back into the house. Marty was thinking about his real parents. "Jason. You think it's time to call the Red Cross?"

Jason was right there. "I don't know, Marty. It seems kind of early to try. They still have shelters up here so far from the Plant. Who knows what's going on down home? I think we need to wait. Also, if one of them is hurt and in the hospital, it will give them time to heal before they have to take care of us again."

"But I miss them, Marty. Don't you?"

"I do. But remember what Dad always said to us. How after a meltdown, everyone had to take care of themselves first? And we're doing that."

"Yeah. But maybe they need us. Maybe they are looking for us. Maybe they have contacted the Red Cross."

"Let's give it a bit and then we will. Come on. We have work to do."

* * *

Mr. Alex was young, perhaps in his late twenties or early thirties. The boys rarely saw him, and he left their money on his kitchen table on Saturdays. His apartment was small but neat and clean and although there was never an adult to supervise them, the boys felt at home while they were there. They related to the dogs with pleasure, enjoyed feeding them, and offering them treats and then taking them on a half hour to forty-five-minute walk.

Alex . . . that's how they referred to him when he was not there . . . left them plastic baggies to use to clean up after the pups. The boys enjoyed walking the dogs and often wound up talking with other people, some of whom had dogs, some of whom did not, but all of whom interacted well with both dogs, neither of whom was vicious.

Moxie would approach a stranger, tail wagging and looking to be petted. Roxie was more sedate but accepted petting by strangers. And on some days, Marty would go to visit his friend and classmate, Ian. As for Jason, he would return to the relief center and wait for Marty to join him for supper after which they watch TV or played cards or WAR. So, the after-school times passed as quickly as did the days.

At the relief center, in late October, Jake, the relief center worker who seemed to be most responsible for them, asked them if they liked blue, green, or red.

"We're getting you some winter coats and hats and gloves. And boots. The coats come in blue, green, and red."

Marty immediately chimed, "Red for me!"

"Either green or blue would be fine," said Jason. "Maybe green."

And so it was they readied for winter, Marty with his red coat and Jason with his green coat and both with black knitted hats, ski gloves, and boots which they donned for school and dog walking or just wandering around the town.

Work at Mrs. Sunderland's became leaf raking and the trimming of low hanging tree limbs after which it was agreed they would come by only if there was freezing rain or snow. When it was to be freezing rain, they spread salt, both before and after. And when there was snow, they shoveled the walk, the steps to the porches, and the drive. But the milk and cookies they always ate outside standing by the table on the porch.

Having given up on calling his home, Jason was resigned to living in the relief center. He and Marty had returned to school in the fall, but when spring came, Marty fell in with a bunch of ruffians and began doing poorly in school and hanging around in the streets after dark. So at the end of the second week of May, especially as neither boy was likely to do well on the upcoming end of year exams, they said goodbye to 'Alex' and Mrs. Sunderland, telling them their family was moving to the country. On Sunday Jason bought two one-way tickets on the train north and on Monday, May 20, 2019, they left Bain for Ellensville which lay just south of Locklee. Unlike Locklee, though larger, Ellensville offered no tourist attraction to bring in transients. So, Jason chose Ellensville because he thought the chance of Marty hooking up with kids headed for trouble might be lesser.

NINE Weekend Visits

September 2018

Mary had scurried around all day, vacuumed, dusted, straightened pillows, and cooked. She would pick up Lou from the rehab around four and Lenore and Carlos were coming over at five thirty. They would have creamed cubed chicken over rice and peas, boiled pear salad, and chocolate cake. All things which Lou liked and could eat without the need for help.

Unescorted, Lou and Mary left the rehab together. Mobility was not a problem for him. She held the passenger side front door open for him and he entered the car, sitting easily. When she reached across him to secure his seatbelt, he prevented her.

"That's okay. I can do it."

Lou's left hand and arm had been gaining strength recently and he remembered to turn his eyes to the left more automatically when things to be done or seen were on his left side. Such was the case with the seatbelt buckle. It clicked in easily for him.

When Lou mentioned the boys, Mary kept quiet as she had led Lou to believe the boys were in Ohio with their aunt. Not that he had asked. It seemed as if they almost didn't exist for him other than in his recollections.

"Nice being out," said Lou.

"Yes. Lenore and Carlos are looking forward to seeing you."

Lou remained silent.

"I've cooked creamed chicken with rice and peas. You like that.

He turned his head to see her. "Yes, I do."

"Everything is green."

"Yes. It's summer. It was April when the Plant went down."

Lou was silent.

"Did you and the boys hunker down?"

Mary held the wheel hard. This was the first time Lou had referred to the past in a question.

Mary thought about it before she answered.

"I did."

Silence.

More silence.

"And the boys?"

"They used the Go-to bag and went north."

They were approaching home. Lou remained silent. Mary did, too.

* * *

The house looked good. Mary had paid Lenore's son, Ricky, to mow the lawn and Mary had kept the bushes trimmed. Mary slipped the key into the door and stood back for Lou to enter. He stood at the door jam. Tears filled his eyes. "When are the boys coming home?"

Oh, God. That question.

"Come on in, Lou." She led him to the couch. They sat, Lou to her left, she to his right.

"Lou, I don't know when they are coming home." "Well, have you talked with them about it?"

"No. I have not."

"Well, I want to see them. Talk to them about it."

Mary looked at her watch. "Oh, my goodness. It's almost five. I have to put the rice on to cook." She rose and headed for the kitchen.

Lou followed her soon thereafter.

"Maybe we could call them."

"Let's wait until after dinner to talk about it." Lou turned and returned to the living room.

* * *

Carlos and Lenore brought flowers. Mary arranged them into a bouquet and placed them on the front recessed windowsill.

"Lou, my man!" Carlos and Lou hugged. Then it was Lenore's turn.

"How nice to see you, Lou! You look great! Especially with all you have been through."

"You're looking well, too, Lenore." Lou was all smiles. It had been a long time since Mary had seen him smile like that.

The dinner went well. Lou sat at the head of the table, Mary on his left from where she could prompt him if he failed to notice her, Lenore on his right, and Carlos, across from him. Mary did not need to prompt him to pass the food to Lenore, but when she needed the cream that sat between Lenore and him, Mary needed to tap his arm to get him to look at her before he attended to her request.

Carlos smiled at Lou. "It's really good to see Mary doing well

now."

"Why? Was she sick?"

"Oh. You don't know.

"Mary, do you want to fill him in?"

"Oh, yes, Lou. It was before I learned where you were. I was sick. Lenore and Carlos took care of me."

"What made you sick?"

So, Mary went with it and Lou turned in his chair to look at her more directly . . . to bring her more into his field of right sided vision.

"Well, Lou, on the day of the meltdown, we were to have lunch together and so I was near the Plant. Suddenly there was an explosion nearby. My window was open. It was such a nice day. And I had my arm on the window edge. A splat of something hit me and looking down I immediately thought "dirty bomb" so I pulled over and cleaned it off."

"It turned out I was right. I discarded my clothes and put on the sweat suit and flip-flops from the trunk, stopped to have the car washed at that solar run place. Luckily, it was open as the grid was down. I could tell it was down because there were no streetlights. And after that, I headed home where I showered and hunkered down. Within the day I knew I was getting radiation sickness. So I went to Carlos and Lenore's and Lenore cared for me for a number of weeks . . . kept me clean and hydrated . . . and fed . . . and gradually I got better and was reassured by the symptoms that there would be no lasting effects."

Mary took Lenore's hand. "I don't know what I would have done without you . . . and Carlos. The phones were out and everyone around was still kind of hunkering down." She smiled at them both.

Lou reached his right hand toward Mary and she took it. "Oh, Mary. I'm so sorry."

After a bit, Lou spoke again. "And what about the boys? Did they hunker down?"

"Well, that is what I was waiting to tell you. When you were ready. When you asked . . .

"When I got home there was a note from Jason. They had left before the threat of fallout was imminent. The note said they had gone north."

"So, when did they return?"

"That's it, Lou. They have not."

“They went straight to your sister’s?”

“No. They did not.” “Where did they go?

“That’s the problem.” “What’s the problem?

“I don’t know where they went.”

After Lenore and Carlos had left, Lou held Mary as she cried and talked about how first she was too sick to worry and when she was better, the phones were not working immediately, but as soon as they were, she had contacted the Red Cross, the police, and her sister. At the same time, she had told them that he, Lou, was also missing. And it had been the Red Cross who had found him so she could see him again at the rehab.

They talked about the resourcefulness of the boys and how Jason would take care of Marty and while it did not mean they were not concerned, they were optimistic that given there was no word at all, the likelihood of their having been hurt or injured was slim.

The boys had made the right decision. Now, all there was to do was wait.

TEN Coming Back

Summer – Fall 2018

Mary had figured out how to control her mourning of the loss of the boys. Mornings she would rise early, drink her coffee in the darkened living room and think about them. She would relive moments with them and imagine them happy and busy someplace north of them. There were small towns and cities in which they might be. She imagined a small town and Jason in charge and the two of them doing odd jobs for money. What she could not figure out, was where they were sleeping. Would it be in a shelter? Had they built a lean-to in the woods? Wherever they were, they were well. She just knew it. And in time, they would all be together.

Days, work in the school was intense and then there were the visits to Lou and still the shopping and housekeeping and regular follow up with the Red Cross online and by phone. And there were the calls to the police who had come to know Mary well. And then there were visits to Lenore and Carlos and their sons. Sometimes Lenore and she would speculate as to how the boys were surviving. They also talked about how accepting Lou was of their not being there. It was strange, but it was a protection for him. Mary wondered if it would pass. And if it did pass, what then?

Nights were different. Sometimes Mary would sleep fitfully, her head filled with a conflagration of mixed dreams. Sometimes she seemed to almost float above the bed. On those nights she woke exhausted and at work walked around between cases in a state of disconnected loss. Gradually, however, the dreams were less invasive and the nights of floating fewer. Mary never imagined them leaving her completely and her only defense was to keep busy days . . . which she did . . . and go to bed tired out. But even that did not work reliably.

Lou was doing well, but his increased impulsivity and left side visual field neglect made it too risky for him to be in anything other than a rehab environment. And given his first rehab was the opposite direction from Mary's place of work, it was arranged that he be moved to one on route between their home and Aesopolis. In that way, when school reopened in September, Mary could go back to work and stop on the way to spend time with Lou.

The team there was wonderful. Once a week, Mary got to attend a team meeting regarding Lou's progress. There they also discussed changes in his treatment plan. For instance, they asked Mary if Lou had a watch at home that she might bring in for him to wear on his left wrist. This, it was thought, would remind him to look to his left when he wanted to know the time. She did that and Lou wore it regularly. And indeed, he did look at it! And without prompting.

In the team meeting, they coached Mary on ways to get Lou to attend more to his left side. They suggested she sit to his left side and to several times in a visit, to touch his left arm when she spoke to him. And it did seem to encourage him to turn his head and look at her there.

Also, as she ate with him, she was encouraged to hand his fork or knife to his left hand to encourage its use. Oddly, this, too, seemed to help although sometimes she had also to say, “Lou, why don’t you try holding your fork in your left hand while you cut?”

And when Lou came home for a visit Friday night through Saturday morning, as he freshened up and dressed, Mary would freshen up beside him and prompt him to hold the washcloth in his left hand or place the toothpaste in it when he reached for his toothbrush. She also would hand his hairbrush to his left hand. And occasionally Lou would reach for the toothpaste with his left hand without prompting. Mary continued to visit Lou at the Rehab weekdays while on Saturday and Sunday, either a physical therapist, an occupational therapist, or a speech language therapist came to the house to do therapy with him. Lou continued to progress physically in terms of left side awareness and use . . . also in terms of ability to attend and sequence, and in his understanding and use of language.

Breakfast he ate with Mary. Lunch a care aide was provided which gave Mary a chance to food shop. Dinner was again with Mary. But except for making himself a cup of coffee or getting food from the refrigerator, Lou was not permitted to use the kitchen for any cooking other than toasting bread in the toaster. And as luck would have it, by the time Lou came home from the rehab unit, his impulsivity had reduced, and he could be trusted to not use the stove.

In building his left arm strength, the PT got him to “use the mush mower” to mow the lawn, and working together, the OT and ST helped Lou build a bird house.

It was Sunday morning. Connie, the speech therapist, and Lou sat at the kitchen table. Before them lay seven labeled pieces of wood: bottom, side, side, side, front, roof, and roof. "Okay, Lou. Here are the pieces you cut out for the birdhouse. Can you show me how they go together?"

Lou picked up a side piece and put a roof piece above it.

"You've got it.

"Except how can you hold them together?

"Let's look at our sequence cards."

The cards read:

> Now screw on the roof.
>
> Place the bottom on the table.
>
> Take a side piece and screw it to the bottom.
>
> Take another side piece and screw that to the bottom and a side.
>
> Screw the front to the two sides.
>
> Now screw on the final roof piece.

Screw the third side to the second side and bottom.

"Which is the first card?"

"The bottom." Lou looked over the sequence sentences and selected, "Place the bottom on the table."

"Which are the next three cards?"

"About the sides."

Lou selected three cards:

Screw the third side to the second side and the bottom.

Take another side piece and screw that to the bottom and a side.

Take a side piece and screw it to the bottom.

“Okay. Now put them in order under the one about the bottom. Look for the hint words. You know . . . like another and third.”

“What do you need next?”

“The front.” He selected:

Screw the front to the two sides.

Lou arranged them as:

Take a side piece and screw it to the bottom.

Take another side piece and screw that to the bottom and a side.

Screw the third side to the second side and the bottom.

“Okay. Now what are left? About the roof.”

Lou selected:

Now screw on the final roof piece.

Now screw on a part of the roof.

Without a prompt he rearranged them to read:

Now screw on a part of the roof.

Now screw on the final roof piece.

“Okay. Let’s do it.”

Lou read the first card and picked up the bottom. He read the second card and picked up a side. He picked up the battery operated screwdriver and a screw and using his right hand to hold the screwdriver and his left to hold the bottom as Connie held the side, he screwed the side to the bottom and proceeding from top to bottom on the list, in a few minutes he had assembled the bird house.

"Nice work, Lou. Now can you take it apart?"

Lou reversed the gear direction and independently working from top to bottom he independently disassembled it.

As he finished the project a sense of satisfaction filled him.

Given his left side neglect, Lou could not mow the lawn or drive the car, however he could use the edger and water the lawn and flowers so while Mary weeded and trimmed the beds, with prompts as to places he had missed, Lou edged and watered.

One day, in preparing Lou's laundry, a small pad fell from his pants pocket. Mary opened it to a list. It ran along the right side of the page. It was titled, "Mowing the Lawn."

It read:

> get the lawn mower out
>
> check the gas
>
> press the starter
>
> go to corner by sidewalk walk along sidewalk
>
> turn at walkway
>
> go along last row mowed do again

Mary realized that Lou had done this on his own . . . in preparation for mowing the lawn. But it had worked. And he did mow it.

Beneath it was a second sheet, “Driving the Car”

open door

get in

close door (on left)

Two Close: A Story of Survival

check right rear-view mirror

check left rear-view mirror

put key in ignition

put car in gear

look right

LOOK LEFT

look in rearview mirror

LOOK LEFT

look in rearview mirror

look right

LOOK LEFT

look right

LOOK LEFT

look right

LOOK LEFT

The list stopped there. It was a start. But he was right. He was not ready. He had perseverated by repeatedly writing LOOK LEFT! look right. He had not driven. Only thought about sequence initially but finally hung himself up with perseveration and his left side neglect problems.

At the center, Lou received intensive therapy five to six times a week for a minimum of three hours and rehabilitation nursing was available 24/7, so the little help that Mary offered was minimal, but coming home boosted Lou's spirits and encouraged him to remain positive. Also, at home he was beginning to show an interest in the computer.

ELEVEN Awakening

Fall 2018 - Spring 2019

Mary had made her usual weekly calls to the Red Cross and the Police and checked the NamUs' online website at www.namus.gov to see if the boys' profiles had been updated as found without her knowledge. Last week she had printed out the posters from the site of Jason and Marty's images, descriptions, and contact information and taken them to Staples where she had had a hundred copies of each printed. These she had shoved into her glove compartment . . . except for the ones she had posted around the mall. Her plan was to post them in the railroad station and to see if she might not also post them in the trains. She figured even if they did not have a regular posting place on them, she could put them up after which they would take them down after which she would put them up again. She was quite sure the boys would have at one point or another used public transportation, either bus or train.

Then of course there was the bus depot where there were bulletin boards and she had posted both boys flyers. Her plan was to return each week to confirm they were still up and if they were not, she would repost them. She had done this without involving Lou. Her thought was that with his lack of awareness of his left side sight, navigating the parking lot and crowds would be too much of a challenge for him.

Mary was glad Lou could see with his full visual field in both eyes. It was just he was not aware of what the left eye saw, although he was beginning to use his left hand more and more recently he was turning his head more frequently to engage her visually when she spoke from his left side. But he still bumped into door jams on his left side. And when he was home on weekends, she did not take him from the house except to walk around the backyard and area below toward the stream . . . but not near the stream as she was afraid he would forget the stream was there and fall in when looking to something of interest on his right. And he also would water the lawn with supervision and on some days with Mary beside him, do its edging. And Mary did take him to the bank for window deposits as he then did not need to descend from the car.

They were on their way to the bank when Lou turned to look at her . . . something new, she thought. He had turned to his left side. Progress.

"Mary, about the boys. What are we going to do to try to locate

them?"

Oh dear. Here it comes, she thought. She kept her eyes on the road.

"Well, I am working with the Red Cross, the National Missing and Unidentified Persons System, NamUs for short, and the police."

"What do they say?"

"After I was feeling better from the radiation sickness and the phones were working again, I contacted them. The Red Cross sent someone to the house . . . as did the police. The NamUs I dealt with on the phone and online. They all agreed that the number of missing persons after the meltdown had skyrocketed in number and that while there were very few horror stories that resulted from their running to escape the risk of fall out and radioactive contamination, about a third of those who had disappeared were still unaccounted for. They all agreed that the shelter system was not as organized as they would like it and they believed that some people had taken to the woods and were just roughing it. Nonetheless, they would do all they could do to track down our boys. And meantime, all we could do was to remain optimistic and wait."

"So, they are not the only ones. I suspected there would be many refugees. They must be in the many thousands."

Lou waited a bit before commenting further. "Yes. Well, Jason has a fair knowledge of survival skills and he would watch over Marty. Maybe they are among those that are just roughing it."

Mary noted the calm with which Lou internalized this information. Perhaps he had suspected such might be the answer. Perhaps he had feared the answer and was relieved that what he heard was so positive. As for herself, this was a new world and as she scanned the papers and listened to the news, she noted there were many stories with happy endings.

Those with the sadder ones had ended soon after the melt down in overrun hospitals and severe radiation sickness.

"But there must be something we can do, Mary."

"We're at the bank now Lou. Maybe on the way home we can stop for some lunch and talk about it."

"Okay. Let's do that."

Mary was happy that Lou's injuries had not after the first few months affected his level temperament. They were lucky in that as Mary knew that often brain damage resulted not only in deficits in logical thinking but also in uncontrolled outbursts of anger. Also, Lou's impulsivity had lessened markedly.

* * *

Mary pulled the car into the parking lot of the Gary Diner. She descended quickly as Lou fiddled to loosen his seatbelt and hurried to the passenger side. It was important that she ensure his loss of left side awareness did not result in his bumping into things or walking in front of a car. She had taken to walking on his left side and holding his hand and touching his arm when she wanted to get his attention to talk to him. He was already opening the car door when she arrived at it.

Lou descended from the car and closed the door with his right hand, banging his left shoulder as he did so. "Damned door!" he said.

Mary caught his left hand and they walked together up the stairs and into the diner. He opened the door on the right just as Mary opened the one on the left . . . which surprised him when it came into view. Mary smiled with recognition of what had happened. But at least he had not bumped it.

They seated themselves in an empty booth and a waiter brought the menus.

Lou ordered a grilled cheese and tomato sandwich, a good choice as he would not have to use a knife and fork . . . just a fork. Mary had a salad. They both had unsweetened iced tea.

"So, Lou. Let me tell you what I've started doing." Mary explained about the flyers. Lou liked the idea. He wanted to help. Mary thought on it.

"Well, what I thought you might do is check the NamUs website for updating and email copies of the posters to people we know. Also, perhaps you might post them on some of the social networks. As for going to the train and bus stations, because of your left side unawareness, I thought it safer if I handle them. You can ride with me to them, but it would probably be safer if you waited in the car until your left side unawareness is better."

"Well. We could do that."

And so, they ate in quiet. And when Lou finished the right side of his sandwich, Mary asked him for his left hand, which he extended to her after which she put it on the left half of his sandwich. This caused him to look down and with his left hand he changed it to his right one and finished eating it. As the tea had been moved to his right side, he had no trouble finishing that.

* * *

Computer use posed its own problems. Primarily Lou used his left hand except for *shift* and *control alt delete*. And to use it for them, he had to remind himself, left hand. Also, he shifted the keyboard to the right . . . which still did not mean he saw the left of it better consistently. But he had no place to go. No clock to punch and so he worked slowly. Over the weeks he began to use his left hand for *tab* and *caps lock* and sometimes he would just use his left hand and watch it with his right eye as he typed the letters on the keyboard. And over time he found he could use it without prompting with the phrase left hand.

The good part was that he could still read, particularly if the font were in narrow columns on which he placed to his right side or worked to turn his eyes to the left as well as right. At any rate, hoppity skippidy he was able to send out copies of his sons' posters to everyone he knew and to post them on Facebook and Twitter.

Then one day early in the New Year, Lou received a response on Facebook from someone who worked in a store up the river toward Bixby who said that he had seen the two boys frequently last summer at his place where they came to purchase food and fishing line. They had been around a number of weeks, but he had not seen them in a few months now. He said he had just figured they were up on a vacation. But he said he would ask around.

Mary contacted the police in the area. They knew nothing.

But they had survived and had been doing well!

* * *

Mary and Lou decided to drive north to the area where the boys had been spotted. They took with them a few posters and tacked them up on store bulletin boards and in the police station. And as by then Lou was more regularly using his right field of vision to scan to the left and had a better sense of sequence and time than he had had a few months back, although he was still not ready to drive, they also went knocking on doors.

"Have you seen these boys?"

"No. Sorry. I haven't"

And at the next house, "Have you seen these boys?"

"No. Sorry. I haven't"

Given Lou was doing better seeing things on his left, he was less of a worry to Mary. Also, the area's population was low so there was little traffic to worry about.

Mary and Lou returned to the area on several weekends. Winter had arrived but there were still some houses they had not canvassed. Christmas came and went.

They knocked on the door of a somewhat tumbledown house. An old man answered the door.

"Yeah?"

"Hi. I'm Mary and this is Lou . . . Matters . . . Mary and Lou Mat-

ters."

"Name's Hank. What can I do ya' fer?"

"We were looking for our sons. Jason and Marty Matters." Mary held up the poster with Marty's picture and Lou held up the one with Jason's.

"Oh, yeah." His voice was low and a bit gruff. "Oh, yeah. I know'em"

"Really?"

"Yeah. Thems the ones I picked up down near Ariana. They wuz hitchin' a ride north to join their father."

"When?"

"Oh, that was back in May. What I didn't know at the time wuz that there had been a mel'down at Magdum Heights. I dunno if they was runnin' from it or no."

Mary was doing the talking. "Where'd you take them?"

“Oh, I dropped them off at the gas station on the main road not far from here.”

“And that was in May?”

“Yep.”

“And that was the last you saw of them?”

“Nope.”

“You saw them again?”

“Yep. Musta bin mid-October.”

“Where were they?”

“They came here. I hadn’t seen them since I dropped them off at the station. But there they were.”

“They came here?”

“Yup. I told them when I dropped them off if they ever needed anything, I lived down the street at number 10.”

“And they came here?”

“Yup.”

“What did they say?”

“Well, they wondered if I would be goin’ to Bixby any time soon.”

“And . . .?”

“I told them I was the next day and to be here in the mornin’ if they wanted a lift.”

“Did they show up?”

“Yup.”

“And did you give them a lift?”

“Yup. Right up to the center of Bixby.”

“Where in Bixby?”

“Right on the main drag. They said their dad lived not far from there.”

“So, you just let them out.”

“Yep.”

“And have you seen them since?”

“Nope. That was it.”

“And that was in mid-October?”

“Yep.”

“Nice boys. Polite. . . Right in the middle. They said they knew their way. Haven’t been up there since what with the winter here and the roads icy.”

“Oh. We understand.”

“Yeah. After the meltdown, gave a lot of people lifts here and there. But they seemed to have family they wuz going to.

“Yeah. And I guess they wuz around a while so they musta’ had family here, too.”

Mary and Lou thanked the man and he gave them his name and address and phone number so they could write or call him.

After Lou and Mary left, they went to the police station and told the police the story and they said they would stop by and talk to Hank. Just in case he had more information.

"Good guy, Hank. Hank Handly. Hard worker. Good neighbor. Probably did give them a lift. He never did mind picking up hitch hikers . . . although we had warned him against it."

They also gave the police copies of the boys' posters and their own names, address, and phone number.

* * *

Mary and Lou returned home in a state of mixed elation and fear. Elation to have word of their sons being alive and well. Fear as to what had happened to them since October, it being mid-winter and the New Year.

On return home, Mary took to the phone and Lou to the computer. Mary called the Red Cross and the police with updates and Lou checked out and had the boys' profiles amended as to where they were last seen. He also sent out emails to everyone he knew and posted updates on the social media.

And Mary called Lenore.

"Lenore, can you believe it? We've heard news of the boys. They were identified as traveling together in a small town north and west of here and last seen on the main street of Bixby."

"Oh, Mary. I'm so happy for you! When was that?"

A sinking feeling hit Mary in the pit of her stomach. "Mid-October."

A silence followed.

Lenore spoke first. "Oh. Well, Bixby. Sounds good. I understand they set up many shelters for those fleeing the meltdown. Perhaps they are in one of them."

"Yes. Well, I contacted the police and the Red Cross. And Lou has notified missing persons at NamUs."

"Well, all you can do is pray and hope. I'm sure you will hear more soon."

Mary hung up the phone. She was not as sure as Lenore. And yet there was a glimmer . . .

Lou and Mary sat at the dinner table. They were silent.

Lou spoke first. "Why don't we go to Bixby? We can look for ourselves."

Mary's heart jumped at the thought of it. On the one hand they had discovered the lead that got them to think of Bixby . . . on the other hand, Lou in an urban environment? With his poor safety awareness? Scary. Just scary.

But wait. Maybe Lenore would be willing to go with them some Saturday? Or maybe even Carlos?

And so it was that in early April 2019, with the ice melting and spring around the corner, Lou, Carlos, and Mary headed out to Bixby with Carlos driving, Lou in the passenger seat beside him, and Mary in the back. She had put it off long enough. Lou was becoming more aware of safety issues and he seemed to be scanning for things on his left side regularly. So why not?

They arrived in Bixby around ten o'clock in the morning. The day was bright. The first thing they did was to purchase a map of the city. And the first place they stopped was at the police station.

"Hi. I'm Mary Matters and this is my husband, Lou Matters, and our good friend, Carlos. We are here looking for our sons." Mary brought out the posters with the images of the two boys on them. "We thought you might be willing to let us post them here."

"Sure." The policeman, a middle-aged chap with an Irish look to him took them and studied them carefully. "I see you listed the boys with NamUs. Are they also listed with the police?"

"Yes. And the Red Cross."

"Let me see if I can pull up their names in the computer. . . Yup, there they are. Here from Ariana, eh? What makes you think they might be in Bixby. Been a long time since they disappeared."

"Well, a man reportedly gave them a lift to here sometime in mid-October. We only found out about it a bit ago. But we understand you have a number of shelters in Bixby and we were hoping we could get their addresses and telephone numbers from you."

"Good idea. Yeah. There are lots of shelters. We have the largest ones listed, but I think there are others that are not on our list." The officer clicked a bit in the computer and the printer printed out a page and a half of shelters names, addresses, and telephone numbers. "Let me give you this."

Mary and Lou looked down the page. There must have been thirty listed. Who'd have thought?

They thanked the officer who said he would hang the posters and left.

By then it was nearing 11:30. "Why don't we sit a bit, make a plan, and eat?" It was Carlos who spoke. Mary and Lou agreed. So, the three climbed back into the car.

"Let's park near the center of town. Maybe there is an area with parking meters. We don't want to stay too long."

"Good idea, Mary. As I drive, we can all watch for a good parking spot."

As they neared the center of town, a car pulled out from a metered spot. Lou spotted it. It was on the right side of the road. Carlos broke, backed up, and parallel parked. Mary had some quarters for the meter and not one hundred feet away was a Dunkin' Donuts. Seemed perfect.

They all ordered coffee. Mary got a Veggie Egg White Flatbread; Lou, Ham Egg and Cheese; and Carlos, a Turkey Sausage Flatbread. Mary spread the map on the table. The first thing to do was to find where they were. That done, they began to look for the nearest shelters. Lou found one quite close. They decided not to find all thirty. They would do that at home. They would settle for finding five. When they were finished, they walked out. Mary put four more quarters in the meter by the car. That would give them another hour. The four of them set out on foot for the nearest shelter. It was an old hotel, just down the street.

Carlos had an idea. “Why not ask here which of the shelters on the list are the largest and we go to them first?”

“Good idea,” said Lou. “Yes,” said Mary.

So, they entered the lobby of the hotel-now-a-shelter. An elderly woman behind the desk welcomed them. “May I help you?”

“Yes. If you would. We are looking for these two boys and we wondered if they had ever been here?”

The woman scrutinized the images and read the info on the posters and responded with an apology. “Sorry. Haven't seen them. I'm here six days a week, mornings. If they had come through in the last six months, I would recognize them. We don't get many young'uns. But we do get some.”

“Oh. Well, thank you anyway.”

Carlos spoke up. “Say, we have a list of the shelters in the area and we were wondering if you knew which were the larger and which were smaller."

"Oh, I could help you there. I'm from Bixby and probably know the buildings in which they are housed."

"Wonderful!"

Mary extricated the list and the map from her purse. "Oh. You're from the area. Maybe you could help us locate them on the map, too."

"Sure. Be glad to."

The woman accepted the list and spread the map on the desk before her. "I could mark the larger ones with a star and the smaller ones with a square. Would that help?"

"Oh, yes. Definitely!"

The process took a bit of time and the woman worked silently. And at a certain point, she looked up. "Done!"

They thanked her profusely and looked to see where the nearest star was. It turned out to be only a few blocks away. "I think we had better take the car," said Mary. And they did.

The second shelter was a large, older home. Mary shared the posters and they asked the same questions but no, the boys had not been seen. And so too with the third, fourth and fifth.

But that was enough for one day. Lou was looking tired. Mary was feeling tired. And Carlos still had the two-hour drive home.

In the car, it was Carlos who spoke of their progress. "Well, we have a list of shelters. We have a map. And we have a strategy."

"Yes," said Mary.

"I think we'll find them."

Lou said, “Thank you, Carlos. And thank you for driving. I’m sorry I’m not yet ready to drive. But I will be.

“Yes, you will be, Lou. And we’ll find the boys.” “So next Saturday same plan?” asked Carlos. “Same plan,” answered Mary.

“Same plan,” answered Lou. “But this time we’ll hit six of those suckers instead of five.”

“And over the week, I will call them,” said Mary.

So, over the next five weekends they continued their systematic search. Mary called all the shelters listed. None of them recalled seeing the boys. Still they wanted to be sure so each Saturday they headed north to Bixby. Some Saturdays Carlos was not available, so Mary drove. And when she and Lou walked, she held Lou’s left hand as they made their way around the town. Today was Sunday, May 26, 2019. They would visit the smallest shelters on the list. They started with the one closest to the first they had visited. It was just around the corner from the hotel. Entering they found the revamped store to be among the most depressing shelters they had visited. A coffee counter was on the left and in front of it a desk with a man seated at it.

“Hi,” he said. “I’m Jake.”

“Oh, hi, Jake. We were wondering if you might help us.”

“Sure. What can I do for you?”

“We’re looking for some boys. Our sons.”

“No boys here. Not now. We did have two who stayed the winter with us. But last week they headed north to be with their family.”

“Oh.” Lou was crestfallen, but Mary pushed onward. “They didn’t happen to be these boys, did they?” “Well, by jum, that’s them. Jason and Marty. Right?”

"Right."

"They were here since fall. Social worker even enrolled them in school. And after school they kept themselves busy walking two dogs. And on weekends, they mowed lawns and trimmed flower beds. And in the winter, they put down deicer and shoveled. Nice boys. Marty was a blast at times. But Jason kept him in tow."

"And they are not here now?"

"Nope. Like I told you. Cleared out last Monday. Said they were going north to join their family. Which was good to hear as according to Marty, Jason had given up calling home last spring as at first the phone didn't answer and then it didn't pick up."

"Oh, dear. That must have been while I was sick . . . and the phones were down . . . and they came back on, but I wasn't there to hook up the answering machine. It was after the meltdown. I had radiation sickness and their dad was hospitalized and his whereabouts unknown."

"Awful sorry. . . do they have people up north?"

"Not that we're aware of. But they were all right? Not sick. Not hurt. And going to school?"

"Nope. They were fine. I kinda miss'em. They were a bright spot in the day. Liked'em both. Nice boys."

"So where do you think they went?"

"Well, I'm not sure. But they said north. And as neither of them is old enough to drive, I would guess they hopped a train. They probably had the money for the tickets from what they earned dog walkin' and mowin'. Like I know Jason bought the two of them cell phones at the 7/11 store so they could keep in touch. And they had warm coats and hats and gloves that we gave'em so even if they wound up in some little mountain town north of here, they would be safe."

Mary and Lou thanked them profusely and left their names and telephone numbers in case they showed up again. They also left the posters with the boys' images and information on them.

Back in the car, Mary wondered aloud. "What should we do now, Lou?"

"Well, I think we should tell the local police. No?"

"Good idea." They headed to the same station they had gone to the first time and found the same policeman sitting desk. They shared with him their latest news and he suggested they go to the bus station and the railway station and post the posters in case anyone saw them in either locale. And he added what they told him to the boys' missing persons' files and told them they would call if they heard anything further. He also said he would alert the police along the rail line to be on the watch for them.

Mary and Lou thanked him and left.

The bus station and the rail stations were close and with Mary holding his left hand, Lou and Mary navigated the parking lots well, posted the flyers, and headed back home. It had been a short day, but a very full one.

Mary drove Lou back to the rehab. They would eat together and then she would leave. Sundays went quickly and Mondays arrived too soon.

At the rehab, Lou's speech language pathologist came in just after they arrived.

"Hi, Mrs. Matters. Nice to see you."

"Yes. And nice to see you, too, Charlotte."

"Hi, Lou."

"Hi, Charlotte."

"Well, I'm glad you are both here. I have good news for you."

"Really?"

"Yes. We are thinking that Lou can begin to spend Monday, Wednesday, and Friday at home. We'll just take it one day at a time, but if that works, we will then think about his living at home full time."

Mary was a bit taken aback by that idea. "You really think he is ready?"

"Yes. Well, he will continue with OT and ST twice a week each at home and PT once a week, but we think he is ready. His sense of time is good now; his sense of sequence has returned; and by and large he is scanning visually for items on his left. His main area of weakness is in the understanding of idioms and second meanings. But that should not affect his ability to keep safe, care for himself, and navigate at home."

"Oh. I'm a bit taken aback. But then you are right. He does seem to be handling himself well. For instance, we've been going to Bixby on weekends and although I still have him hold my hand, I now rarely have to watch what he is up to in order to keep him safe."

Mary laughed aloud. "Oh, my goodness, Lou. Perhaps I have been babying you too much."

"I love it when you baby me, Mary." And he gave her a big hug after which he smiled warmly, looking into her eyes.

"Yes, so you can pick him up either Sunday night or Monday morning. Your choice."

“Oh, I’ll pick him up on Sunday.” “Around seven?”

“Yes. After dinner. Around seven.”

TWELVE To North Country

May 2019

The railroad station in Bixby was large and old but beautiful. Jason and Marty entered it and its size, the height of its ceiling and its openness near took their breaths away. They looked at one another and Jason gave Marty a nudge. "Let's look like we've been here before."

"Let's go to the men's room, Jason. See. Over there?"

They headed toward a sign hanging from the ceiling: Rest Rooms. No one was in the rest room so the two of them spoke freely.

"I'm hungry, Jason."

"Okay. So, let's head to that restaurant we saw on the right when we came in. We'll get a table near the windows so we can check out the lay of the place. Then we'll purchase a ticket north."

"Let's pick up train schedules on the way. I think I saw them in the box on the counter of the island in the middle."

"Good idea."

"Hey, Jason. Did you hear about the absent-minded man who went to the urinal, opened his vest, pulled out his tie, and pissed in his pants?"

Jason gave Marty one of his I don't believe it looks. They did their business, washed their hands, and left.

Once outside, Marty led the way to the center island. "Good morning. May I help you?"

Jason spoke. "We were looking for some train schedules to travel north."

"Right here." The clerk handed Jason a schedule from the box on the counter.

"May I have one, too?"

The woman handed one to Marty.

Somehow Marty had bought into Jason's idea of waiting until "things were better." He no longer mentioned calling the Red Cross and seemed enmeshed in his own life. Jason could not tell what Marty thought about the past, but one thing was certain. Even if he didn't mention it, he still had his parents in mind because before all else, Marty was steadfast and relentless in his love and respect . . . even for Jason . . . and that was how Jason knew Marty had not forgotten. He was just waiting.

Sitting in the restaurant beside the window, they ordered eggs and ham to eat there and sandwiches to go. While they waited, they inspected the inside of the train station. There were a row of numbered ticket windows, but it being past rush hour, there were no lines. The boys finished their breakfasts and drank their juice and milk. Jason insisted they have milk daily and Marty liked milk and felt responsible drinking it. But for the road they ordered two cans of soda each which, along with the sandwiches, they shoved into their backpacks.

The train's last stop before Canada was a town called Locklee. They bought tickets to it. The ride with stops would be four hours. They would arrive in the early afternoon.

They boarded the train and took seats on opposite sides of the isle so they each were near a window. The car was near empty; talking across the space between them would be fine. And if the car began to fill, Marty would move to beside Jason on the river side of the ride.

"Marty. I think we should turn our cells off. I'm not sure when we will be able to charge them again."

Marty replied by taking his backpack from the seat in front of him, pulling out the phone, and holding the button down until it closed down, after which he returned it to the pack.

The two rode in silence, each looking out his window, watching the countryside slip by as they went further and further into the mountains. At a certain point the river disappeared and a while thereafter the train made a stop at Ellensville. The boys descended. A small hot dog stand was near the station so they each got a chili hot dog and a soda. The railroad station was merely a platform with roof over it and two yellow porta potties. They each used one and struck off on the road north where the sign read Locklee.

They headed into the woods as they had planned, and about a mile in from the road, Jason opened their newly purchased tent described as: SKYLINK Starhome Lightweight 2 Person Camping

Backpacking Tent with Carry Bag. This would be their home while the scoped out the area and came up with a better plan. They had tins of fish, crackers, peanut butter, and jelly. They would purchase drinks at the store and pick berries in the woods. And Marty would not be around the street kids with whom he had gotten into petty thievery.

Their plan worked for several days until a series of thunderstorms hit the area and ground became wet and they no longer felt safe.

"Let's hop a train for Locklee. See if in a smaller village we can find a niche."

And so, they did. They packed, headed for the train station, purchased tickets at the ticket sales window, and twenty minutes later the conductor called, "Locklee, next stop."

To their surprise, the land between the train station and the lake was a wall to wall shanty town. From where they stood, they could see gardens starting and people coming and going among the many put-together homes. A nod from Jason and they headed inland.

"Wow! What is that?"

"Well, I read that the refugees from the melt down had moved north for safety and that many had established camps and homes in North Country. I think that is what we were looking at."

"Yeah."

"I just didn't realize how many there would be!"

"No wonder we don't know what happened to Mom and Dad." Neither of the boys ever talked of their parents; it was exceptional that Marty would even make that observation. "Yeah," said Jason.

"Yeah," said Marty.

The railroad station was a good walk from the main road which lay to its west. Jason and Marty padded along the path to it in silence. They had no plan. They would have to develop one.

From the street signs they learned that the main road was ROUTE 3 N and entrance to it from the station lay south of the town of Locklee. They started to walk north. No view of the town was in sight, but they came to a small side road that went off to the left.

“Why don’t we see what’s up this road?” asked Jason. “Maybe we can find a place to camp out for the night.” “Yeah.”

The road only had two houses on it. They were small. Almost cabins. They passed the first one and went on to the second one. Except for a squirrel or a bird flying overhead, the area was quiet. No traffic. And no cars or trucks parked by the cabins.

They walked around the cabin. Marty knocked on its door. No answer. Jason went around the side and back of it. No one.

Jason headed toward the east side of the house, but a dog appeared from the bushes suddenly, setting up a barking ruckus.

Marty had spied a small window propped open on the east side of the house. A rain barrel stood below it. He had hitched himself up and just a Jason appeared around the house from the back and the dog came out of the bushes, Marty waved goodbye and dropped out of sight into the cabin as Jason grabbed a stick and gave it a swing toward the dog that was still twenty feet away from him.

Well, he had to take care of the dog first. So, Jason decided to befriend him. He reached into his pocket where he had stashed the last bite of his sandwich . . . in case he was to need it. He took it out and threw a piece of it to the dog who sniffed it and gobbled it down. He threw the other piece of it and while the dog ate that, picked up a small stick with which he might play fetch.

"Fetch!" he called and threw the stick. The dog went for it. And not only did he pick it up, he brought it to Jason, sniffed him, and even let Jason pet him.

Jason waved the stick in the air well above the dog. "Fetch!" he cried, and the dog ran after the flying stick. Jason moved closer to the window. And at about that moment, a man pulled up at a slight distance, stopped, and descended from the truck, being careful not to trigger his readied shotgun.

"Mornin'. How you boys doin'?"

"Pretty good," the older boy answered.

"I'm Lem," Lem offered and held out his hand.

The boy accepted it. "I'm Jason. Nice to meet you, Lem."

"Say, Jason, do you think you could get your brother out here?"

"Yeah. Sure." He turned toward the open window. "Hey, Marty! You can come out now."

Marty raised his towhead above the sill of the window. He looked to be somewhere between eight and ten years of age.

"Whatcha' doin' there, Marty?" asked Lem. "Cleaning." Marty always had an answer.

"Cleaning out, you mean," suggested Lem. "Cleaning out the refrigerator."

"Yeah." Marty appeared nonplussed. "Something like that."

"Well, Marty, suppose you get yourself out here and pick up this stuff and put it back where you got it. My friends would miss it when they got back if you didn't."

"Whatcha' going to do with us?" asked Jason as Tufty approached to restart the play.

“Well, first I’m gonna’ to take you down to my house and give you each a bowl of soup. And second, I’m gonna’ take you down to the Red Cross station so they can arrange for you to get your next meal.”

Jason looked up from petting Tufty. Relief filled his face. “Really?”

Lem just stood there. “Really.”

“Maybe I’d better go help Marty. Make it faster.”

But Lem was not that trusting. “No. You stay right there. You got the benefit of the doubt from me this time. But not that much benefit. I figure you and your brother are just hungry kids looking for a handout . . . but I didn’t say I knew it to be true. So you can just stand there thinking about how you are going to explain to me how you were an accomplice in breaking and entry into my best friend’s home and how as the older brother you set your younger brother up to become a thief.”

Thaw and Natalie, the owners of the cabin they had broken into, returned home that night to a full refrigerator and May, Lem’s sister, got to serve the potential thieves a meal. And the potential thieves reported being separated from their parents who commuted to work in a town near Magdum Heights. According to the older brother, Jason, the mother worked as a speech pathologist in the schools in Aesopolis and their father worked as an engineer at Magdum Heights. Calls to their respective work numbers by Jason had received non-working number responses. This was the same with their home.

According to the boys, when the Heights went down, they were repairing a bike in the basement of their home. Suddenly the ground shook beneath them. Emerging from where they were, they discovered fires in the distant south. As it was unclear as to how close or far they were, or what might have been their cause, Jason had ordered Marty to fill his school backpack with cans of food and a large bottle of water. He had done the same but also included two forks, a sharp knife, a can opener, and a roll of toilet paper. Jason then had ordered Marty to don a sweat suit with a hood over his clothes in case the weather turned cold or they wound up sleeping outside. The two of them then took off for the main road where a truck driver picked them up and took them perhaps thirty miles north. After this it was more difficult getting a lift but in the first truck, they had learned from the trucker's two-way radio that Magdum Heights had gone down. This had confirmed Jason's greatest fears. Saying nothing of the implications of what Jason mentally also referred to as "the event" to Marty, the two of them had continued to hitch all the way to Bain where they had managed to find room in a shelter in which they subsisted until the winter broke. In the telling, Jason omitted telling of their having lived in the woods in the abandoned house. But Jason, having gathered enough information to pretty much confirm he would never see his parents alive again, and not yet ready to return to view the devastation or lack thereof of their locked but abandoned home, at a certain point had determined to push northward, away from the city and away from the crowded shelter where emigrants and Bain street people slept mixed in a crowded room containing twelve cots.

Lem was impressed . . . and interested. It was quite a story. "How'd ya find livin' in the shelter?"

"Well, I got Marty a cot next to mine, close enough so I could reach over in the night to be sure he was safe. It wasn't bad. And Marty and I were company for one another."

"Yeh," said Marty. "Jason found us ways to earn money. We walked dogs, mowed lawns, and shoveled. And sometimes we'd sweep for the stores."

Marty didn't mention his playing in the alleys and streets of Bain and wandering in and out of stores for warmth and safety. And Jason omitted the part about how by mid-winter, Marty had become quite facile at helping himself to small items such as gloves and caps and candies and crackers with peanut butter or cheese on them which he stored beneath his mattress for rainy days. And, yes, Jason had been able to pick up a bit of cash now and then, walking dogs, mowing lawns. washing store windows and shoveling snow with a shovel he had bought with some of his lawn mowing money.

"Yeh. Jason used the money he earned for things we needed . . . sliced ham . . . soap."

Jason did not mention that around Christmas, he spied Marty's stolen stash beneath his mattress or how he reprimanded him, started him on an allowance, and bought him a shovel, too, so he could earn his own money when it snowed, which it did rather frequently but never heavily that year.

"Just come spring, we decided to leave for hill country. So, I bought us train tickets north to Ellensville." Jason did not tell about how they had camped in the woods for a few days in a pop-up tent he had purchased in Bain and survived on wild berries, vegetables stolen from gardens, and fish Jason bought in town until he bought a cheap fishing pole and could catch his own. Or how when the storms came they took the train north to Locklee which is how they came on that day to be where they were as in their wanderings they stumbled onto Thaw's property and found it ripe for picking.

Marty was petting Tufty. He recalled how the pup had been anything but ferocious, and how one of the windows in the empty house had been left raised to let in the breezes from the lake. Cutting the screen had not been a problem, but then Lem had presented himself and so it was that they had landed in the best place possible, given their situation.

About then, May, Lem's sister, called them for dinner . . . reheats as their mom would have called them. And after dinner, Lem took them down to the Red Cross station and arrangements were made for them to live temporarily in a shelter. And there, the Red Cross, after careful questioning, managed to identify and locate their maternal aunt, Leanora Stykes, who lived in Ohio.

After talking with Leanora on the phone, the Red Cross lady arranged that the two boys be shipped off to stay with her and her husband, Bob, with a stipend to be provided by the Ohio county that would list them as foster children. There they would attend school and return to a more normal lifestyle, orphans still, but no longer on the road and without proper food, housing, and schooling. There they would live parentless but better provided for than many of the children in Ellensville where, due to the overcrowding issue, the kindergarten through high school building remained only half available as a school, the other half was being utilized as a shelter.

THIRTEEN News

May 26, 2019, Sunday

For the first time, given the Monday-Wednesday-Friday plan for Lou to be home, Mary did not return him to the rehab when they returned from their trip to Bixby. He would sleep in the house and she would leave him there when she went to work in the morning and drive him back after school on Monday.

Lou was tired so Mary suggested he take a nap which he did. She tucked him in and went downstairs.

The phone rang and she picked it up.

"Mary! It's me." It was Leanora, her sister in Ohio.

"Oh, L'nora. How are you?" Leanora sounded either stressed or excited. She wasn't sure which.

"I just got off the phone with the Red Cross. They have located

Jason and Marty. And they are sending them here. I know that sounds crazy. But I couldn't think what else to do. What with Lou not well or at home and you working."

"You say they found the boys?"

"And they're all right?"

"Yes. They are fine. What should I do?"

"Well, their coming to you would be all right. But l need to talk to the Red Cross first and I'll let you know. Do you have a number?"

"Well. Let me explain."

"Yes?"

"They think the boys are orphaned and it was all so much, I didn't get chance to explain. I need to call and get it all straightened out. But they had this elaborate plan in place and I just was so taken aback that I just figured as the boys were okay, I would let it be and talk with you first. But I was thinking. I think it is a good idea for the boys to come here. What with Lou in rehab and you working? And maybe you could come out, too. After school closed.'

"Well, I'll have to talk to Lou about it. Meantime, if I had the Red Cross number . . . and you could call them and call me back when they have the full picture and then I could call and maybe talk to the boys."

"Sounds like a plan."

Leanora gave Mary the number and they hung up.

From the Red Cross shelter, the Red Cross worker again called Leanora. "Mrs. Stykes, the boys are not with me now, so I wanted to talk more to you. Privately."

"Yes."

"Do you know anything about the boys' parents?"

"Well. Yes. And that is what I wanted to tell you. Except today was so unexpected and you already had a plan in place, so I didn't get a chance to talk with you."

"Oh. Sorry. Please tell me."

"Well, both parents suffered injuries because of dirty bombs. Mary was sprayed with radioactive materials and got radiation sickness. Lou was thrown by the blast of a dirty bomb and suffered head and bodily injuries that left him with fractured ribs and a closed right side head injury. But it is the head injury for which he is still in a rehab unit. Mary, on the other hand, is better and has gone back to work."

"Oh, dear!"

"But Lou is making progress. Initially he suffered from amnesia and as he was unidentified, he remained in the hospital and his whereabouts unknown to Mary. Except about the time Mary became better from the radiation sickness, Lou recalled his identity and they were reunited. Well, so to speak. He of course remains in the rehab. Mary had returned to their home and soon thereafter returned to work."

"Yes."

"So the situation is that perhaps it is best they come to live with me, Leanora, Mary's sister, and Bob Sykes, my husband in Ohio then Mary can join them when school closes . . . she's a speech pathologist in Aesopolis . . . and as Lou is just this week starting to come home three days a week, possibly he would be able to join them, too."

"Sounds like a plan. But I need to talk to the boys' parents." "I gave Mary your number, and she is going to call you." "All right. I'll wait.

And thank you."

* * *

"Hello. Yes. This is Mary Matters. I am calling about my sons . . . Jason and Marty."

"One moment please . . . Oh, yes. Jason and Marty . . . Matters,"

"My sister, Leanora, called me to tell me they had been located and that they are being sent to her in Ohio. Could I confirm that?"

Many questions and verifications later, the Red Cross worker confirmed that was the plan.

"Is there any chance I might talk to them? The boys?"

"Well, yes. It just so happens they are in our lay over rooms. I will get them."

It seemed like an eternity before the worker returned. "Yes. Mrs. Matters. I have Jason and Marty here. I've put you on speaker phone so you can all talk."

"Mom?" It was Marty.

"Hello, Marty. How are you? I've been so worried."

"Us, too. We're fine." "Jason. Are you there?

"Yes, Mom." There was a catch in his voice. "Good to hear your voice."

"Where's Dad, Mom? Is he all right?"

"Yes, Marty. In fact, I hear him coming down now. We had been to Bixby. Looking for you. For both of you."

Mary called to Lou to come down. She had good news. Lou entered the room. He looked as if he had been sleeping. Hair awry. Eyes heavily lidded.

“What’s up, Mary?”

“It’s the boys. They are on the phone.”

“On the phone?” Lou snapped to alertness.

“Yes, on the phone.”

“Where are they?”

“They are with a Red Cross worker. You can talk to them. They are on speaker phone.”

Mary put the phone on speaker phone. Lou spoke first.

“Jason? Marty?”

“Hey, Dad. How are you?” asked Marty.

“Oh. I’m good. And you?”

“I’m fine. And so is Jason.”

“Hey, Dad.” It was Jason.

“Jason! How wonderful to hear your voice . . . both your voices.

“When are you coming home? Are we coming to pick you up?”

“Well, that’s what we are figuring out. We thought you and Mom were gone . . . as in really gone . . . so we gave the Red Cross Aunt Leanora’s and the plan was for us to go to her place in Ohio.”

“Oh. Really.” He gave Mary a frantic, questioning look.

“Yes,” said Mary. “Well, that is what we have to talk about. Whether or not that is a good plan. However, school closes in a couple of weeks and it might be good to just go out there . . . all of us . . . and relax and enjoy one another on the farm. And Leanora would be happy to have us, I know."

* * *

"Well, maybe we can facetime them. Do you think Leonora and Bob have internet?"

"Oh, they do. Leonora and I email each other . . . when we are too busy to call or the news is minimal."

Lou's response was not a real surprise to Mary; however, she was sure that if it had been before his injury, he would have argued for her to go and him to stay. But this was the new Lou and his only response was, "So for now, we have nothing we need to do."

They cleared away the dishes and Lou suggested they play Rummikub.

Mary put the box with the board game in it on the dining room table. Lou seated himself across from her. She placed the flat sheet of plastic they used to play on the table, distributed the blue cube holders, and held the chips bag open for Lou to choose one. He chose an eight after which she chose a nine. "I guess I go first," she said. She picked fourteen chips from the bag and arranged them in the holder. Lou did the same. It was good to see him spontaneously reach to take the bag from his right hand with his left so he could count out fourteen. The first times they had played this after the accident, she had to hold the bag while he took them out. But gradually he had responded to the question, "Where's you left hand?" But now he used it spontaneously.

Mary's thoughts drifted. She would call her sister when they finished the game. She'd talk to her about Facetiming.

Lou's number sense had remained strong except in sequencing. When they first had played the game, Mary had to help him find the sequences. Adding to come up with thirty or more total so he could open was not a problem once the sequences were recognized. Now, however, he recognized the sequences and sets spontaneously and could open without help. Winning, however, was yet to happen. But this too did not seem to faze him.

Early on, Mary would help him look for ways to use the tiles on the board to merge with his own. But now, he did it independently. It occurred to Mary she should tell that to his speech therapist. She'd be impressed.

Mary played the game with only half an eye, but Lou was on task. He re-arranged the tiles on the board and by mixing his and those on the board, he created sets of three numbers with some of them and new sequences with others of them.

"Rummikub!"

"Lou. Oh, my goodness. You did it!" Mary rose and came around the table and gave him a big hug. He smiled generously, looked her in the eyes, and kissed her back. This was big!

Mary was sure it would take a couple of weeks to adjust and to have Lou adjust to leaving the rehab. And maybe in two weeks he would be ready to be home full time.

Since his injury, Lou had a rather laid-back manner of acceptance of things as they came. As such he had not hopped on the news of the boys being found and going to Ohio as a must respond to now event. Somehow, he left everything to Mary in terms of setting the family course and planning how to actualize it. On the one hand, Mary missed the old dynamic, decisive Lou she knew before his brain injury, but on the other hand it made it easier for her to think things through without discussion.

As for how Mary felt, she wanted so badly to be near her sons, to confirm they were well, to see how they had matured, to talk with them about their time on their own, she would have left immediately for Ohio . . . or better yet, have told her sister they needed to be put on a plane and flown east as soon as they arrived at the farm . . . except she could not . . . and she did not want to upset Lou . . . although she did not know if he would become upset if she did . . . he was just so accepting of life as it came. As such, Mary wrestled alone with the question.

In bed that night, Mary lay awake long after Lou had drifted off.

Mary's years as a clinician sorting what could be done from what could not be done in terms of patient expectations had strengthened not only her skill in analysis, but also her skill in keeping her feelings under cover and dealing rather objectively with what could be done rather than what she would like to see happen. And at this time her family was the patient . . . broken, healing, separated, but not without hope. As such Mary reviewed the scene. Lou could not be left alone. Lou still required maintenance. He could not drive. She could not leave him if she went to Ohio. Her sister and brother-in-law were confident and caring people. They had all grown up in extended farm families in the Midwest. In such families, it was not unusual to have a child stay with another wing of the family when there was trouble. Most often it was because the kids were in trouble. Perhaps they had fallen in with a rough gang or one of their parents had become ill or had separated from the family. So, in a sense, this was Mary's situation now. Lou needed care. And the boys must need much TLC. Her sister and brother-in-law could provide that. School was closing so there was no sense in their returning. They probably had outgrown their clothes and a major shopping spree would be required along with their return to school . . . as well as the purchase of school supplies. And with the school year drawing to a close, and all the end of the year reports being due, Mary could not go on leave . . . her professional identity was just too strong to permit it. After all, the boys were alive and well after a year on their own, what difference would a couple of weeks make? Also, given Mary was the main wage earner for the family now, it seemed important she keep her personal days for emergencies, and leave without pay would tighten their finances causing greater stress and anxiety. Mary reviewed the picture numerous times. The only thing to sacrifice in waiting was Mary's having her desire to see Jason and Marty met ASAP. Mary's decision was clear and final. They would wait until school closed.

The day had been full, and Mary had decided to wait until evening to talk with Lou about the need for them to make a plan. They sat in their kitchen over coffee. They had finished dinner and it was time to talk. They needed a plan. The question was when would they go to Ohio and how would they travel?

"Well, Lou, I think we should wait until school closes. It is only a few more weeks. And perhaps by that time the rehab will say you are ready to leave it. If necessary, we can line you up some therapy in Ohio. Or maybe we will find that all of us at home will be enough."

"Mary. I can wait. You go."

"Lou, I can't. I need to finish the school year."

Lou was silent.

"And I can't leave you. Not when you have come so far. And not that you can come home in the week."

And so, it was that that became the plan.

FOURTEEN Ohio Here We Are

Late June 2019

The Red Cross worker . . . his name was Hicks . . . drove Jason and Marty to the Bixby airport, put them in the safekeeping of a willing stewardess, and bade the boys goodbye. They were on their way to Dayton, Ohio, where their Aunt Leanora and their Uncle Bob would pick them up and transport them to their farm that lay just outside of Springfield. The boys understood they raised winter wheat, corn, and alfalfa and in lesser amounts, cucumbers, string beans, tomatoes, lettuce, and pumpkins for the family. The boys had been to visit them a few years back and all they could remember was the cows . . . at that time there were only two . . . the barns, and the freedom.

In the plane, Marty got the window seat as he was shorter and Jason could see most anything he needed to by just leaning closer toward the view. They belted themselves in and sat back. Riding in a plane was new to them.

Jason pulled out the safety instructions folder from the pocket behind the seat in front of him. Marty followed suit. The speakers in the plane came on. The stewardess spoke. “We are preparing for takeoff,” she announced. “Please put your tables up and your seats in a vertical position.” Then she demonstrated the life saving techniques outlined in the brochures the boys had perused. Luckily, they weren’t sitting next to an emergency exit.

The steward pushed along a cart with soda and water in it. “Nuts or cookies?”

Marty chose cookies, Jason nuts.

Marty gave the steward a broad smile. “Hey. Did I tell you about how my girlfriend and I often laugh about how competitive we are?” He paused. “But I laugh more.”

The steward slapped him a high five. “You got it, Man!” And he gave Marty a second package of cookies.

* * *

The trip was by way of Washington, D. C. . . . which made it special. They had a chance to look down on the Capitol and its surrounding monuments. And to see the Potomac. They did not leave the plane and were off again in twenty minutes. The complete flight was under four hours. Amazing!

When the boys deplaned at the Dayton International Airport, an airlines worker accompanied them to the exit where they found their aunt and uncle eager to see them and waiting.

“Oh, my goodness! You’ve grown so much!” Leanora and Bob took turns hugging them. As they only had their backpacks, there was no need to wait so they headed for the parking lot and settled in for a ride to the farm. Dayton looked big, but it was not long before they were outside of the city limits with broad fields of young and sprouting grains. The sky looked bigger out here. And the air had a farm aroma to it.

After about twenty minutes, they pulled into a long dirt road that led to a large rambling farmhouse they recognized as being their aunt’s and uncle’s. To the right was a barn and two silos and to the left, a large vegetable garden. Eight or ten cows grazed in the nearby field and some chickens ran around inside a wire fence a bit to the right and behind the house. Yup. This was it. A feeling of being home settled over the boys. They were excited, but for the first time in a year or so, they felt safe . . . off alert . . . among their own. A feeling of warmth and love flooded Jason. Aunt Leanora reminded them a lot of his mom.

* * *

Jason and Marty shared an upstairs bedroom. The weather was pleasant and the temperature in the low seventies, so they opened the windows and welcomed the fresh air. It was nearly dinner time. Jason washed up and changed his shirt. Marty followed suit. They headed downstairs.

Leanora was in the kitchen cooking. Bob asked if anyone wanted to go to the barn with him. Marty said he did. Jason said, “I think I’ll just stay here and help Aunt Leanora.”

“Well, isn’t that nice of you, Jason! One can always use a bit of help.”

“Yes. And what can I do?”

“Well, you could begin by setting the table. There will just be the four of us. Cal is still at college, but he’ll be home in a few days. Early June. Just about the time we start harvesting the alfalfa.”

* * *

Bob put Marty to work weeding the vegetable garden and milking the cows. It took a bit for him to learn to attach the milkers.

“First thing ya’ haf’ ta’ do, Marty, is to pull on the utters like you’re a calf nursing. That’ll tell the cow to let down her milk. Next thing is to take one of these towels here and wipe the teats down with iodine. One towel per cow. Wanna’ try it?”

Marty took the towel and swabbed the teats down.

“Okay. So now you have to flip up the claw . . . we call these four milkers the claw . . . and attach them to the teats. First, we press in the stopper here so the vacuum will work. Then we attach them in this order.” Bob demonstrated as he did so. “Back right, front right. Back left, front left.” Marty watched.

“Now we wait four or five minutes and the vacuum will release. For the cow it feels like a calf is drinking because it pulses and releases in turns between two teats at a time.”

When the milkers released, Bob took a hose that looked like it had a milker cup on it. “Okay, now, we dip each teat in this iodine just to prevent any germs from bothering the teats.” He demonstrated by holding a funnel shaped cup on the end of a hose and putting each teat in turn into the fluid in it. “And we’re done. We open the gates and the cow returns to the housing area. She feels comfortable and we have our milk."

"Pretty neat."

"Okay. Your turn."

Marty reached for a clean towel. He did well except for forgetting to put in the stopper and being confused at first as to why the milker did not hold onto the teat. But that only happened the first time. After that he did well.

* * *

That evening, Leonora and Marty played Uno while Bob took

Jason out to look at the fields. Jason found the farm to be larger than he first thought it to be. There were fields of corn just coming up. And of winter wheat that was already headed . . . he learned that meant it had grain seeds already at the top of the stalk . . . and that also would be soon cut. Bob also told him that the alfalfa was almost ready to be cut.

The two went by truck, but at a point, Bob stopped by a tractor and a large machine not far from it. Bob said it was a swather or windrower. He said it was used in place of what used to be the binder. It would be used to cut the wheat and alfalfa. He said it would be attached to a tractor. He pointed out the cutter bar that was driven by the shaft of a tractor. And there was a kind of a reel that would sweep the grain onto a platform and a canvas conveyor which would carry it to one side and deposit it in the windrow . . . also called the swath . . . of the field for drying after which when it was just the right dryness, it would be baled and brought to a central place. Jason was impressed. Who knew farming would be so technical and involved so much planning? For Jason, growing food had meant something like you plant the tomato plant, pick the tomatoes when they are ripe, and pull the plant when the season was over. Oh. And of course, you fertilized and weeded.

And a question rose in Jason's mind. Who repaired these machines when they broke down? And it occurred to him that his uncle knew not only about crops and weather and fertilizing and animal care but also about machines . . . and their repair.

Bob said, "Jason, I'd like to take you for a ride on this tractor, but it will only seat one . . . the driver. And you are not yet ready to drive. Still, I thought you might like ta' climb up and get the feel of it."

Jason climbed up.

"Would you like to drive it?"

Jason indicated he would.

"Well, let me think about it. And talk to your mom about it first."

*   *   *

When Jason and Bob returned to the house, Marty and Leanora had chocolate chip cookies baking in the oven.

"Wadja think, Jason? Of what you saw?" asked Leanora.

"Impressed. Just impressed. I didn't have a clue as to how far your fields reached. Or how complicated it was to manage. And Bob says that maybe I can learn to drive the tractor. If Mom says okay."

"Hey, Jason." Marty had a glint in his eye. "Know how the farmer got his wife?"

“No. How?” Jason figured Marty would be pulling his leg. And he was.

“He tractor down.”

Jason responded with a roll of his eyes, a shake of his head, and a groan. “Only you, Marty, would come up with that.” But they were amused.

“But listen, Jason. Mom called; we’re gonna Skype!”

“Really?”

“Yeah. On the computer. We said we’d call her when you came in. And we’ll be able to not only talk to but see Dad and Mom!”

A laptop was already set up at the end of the kitchen table. Leanora sat at it and brought up Skype. She dialed the number which rang. Lou picked up. Mary stood behind him, reaching over his shoulder and working the controls. When their faces emerged, Jason’s eyes welled, and Marty gave a whoop. “Hey, Dad. Hey, Mom.”

Jason noted his dad looked thinner. As did his mom. And her hair was longer. And neither of them had a tan. But they looked well.

“Hey, Marty.”

It was their dad who spoke first. “Hey, Jason.”

Mary smiled broadly across the miles between them, but tears ran down her cheeks. “Hey, boys. How are you?”

Jason answered. “We’re fine, Mom. And you two?”

His dad answered. “Well, it’s been a bit of a haul, but we’re doing well. Especially now. Knowing you two are safe and well. But it was scary.”

“Tell us about it!” said Marty.

"Hey! But we weathered it!"

"So good to see you!"

"Yes. And we'll be out as soon as school closes."

"Wonderful!" It was Jason. "And maybe by then I'll know how to drive a tractor. Whadaya' think, Mom? Dad? Bob says he could teach me if you said it was all right."

"Well, you're sixteen now. Right?" said his dad.

"Yup."

"Whadaya' think, Mary? Yes?"

"Just as long as Bob is willing, and he is your only teacher."

"Sounds good," said Bob. "And hey, nice seeing you! And the boys. They've grown. And Marty has a way of making us laugh."

"So glad you're there!"

They talked a bit more, but there was so much to tell and share they decided to do it just a bit at a time. And Mary encouraged them both to write. And to phone any evening or on the weekend. And she said their dad would be available days on Monday, Wednesday, and Friday. So, they ended the conversation. And Leonora broke out the cookies and the boys, Bob, and she snacked together in peace and happiness.

* * *

Jason lay in bed thinking about where they were in their lives. The effects of the meltdown had touched them all. He and Marty had been forced to be responsible for themselves. And with luck, they had made it through. Fall would come and they would return home. Perhaps even sooner. And they would return to school. He wondered about his classmates. How had they been affected? Were they still alive? Were there still the teams? Would he play Jayvee again? Would he be able to study as he used to do? And Marty. He'd grown so much. Would he still participate in petty thievery? He would have to ask him.

And Mom and Dad. He understood they had both been ill . . . or hurt. Something about Mom having radiation sickness, and Dad being injured in a blast. Something about right hemisphere brain damage. And left side neglect. Maybe tomorrow he would google about it. Tears of release rolled down his face. Poor Mom. Poor Dad. And as for Marty, he was a tower of strength. And so happy his parents were not only alive but well!

Tonight, however Jason was tired. It had been a full day. And maybe tomorrow he would learn to drive the tractor.

* * *

Marty had had a good day. Seeing and talking with mom and dad had just capped it. Dad looked a little thinner and could use a tan. But they both seemed all right. And Leonora was nice and caring. And she didn't mind that he had beaten her at Uno. And he liked baking. And Bob had taught him how to milk the cows. His plan was to rise early in the morning and head for the barns. It was work, but milking was interesting. And important.

* * *

It was Sunday. Jason had gone down to the barn to watch Marty milk the cows. He was quite proficient at it, patting them on the rumps, working their teats and disinfecting them and attaching the milkers. Jason noted how grown up Marty had become. He sat beside him on a milking stool.

“So. Today we get to Skype with Mom and Dad.”

Marty was cleaning the udder of a cow. “Yup. Sure like Skype.”

“What do you think of how they are, Marty?”

“Well, I think they are well. Dad is quieter than he used to be. And didn’t seem to joke around. But he’s getting tan and has gained weight. Mom seems fine but a bit tired.”

“I see them the same way. Can’t wait for them to come out.” “Me, too.

“I think they’ll be impressed by how much you have grown up.”

“Well, you, too.”

“So, I’ve been thinking.”

“Yeah.”

“What about?”

“Well, about our time in Bixby.”

“Yeah.”

“And how you fell in with that gang of street kids.”

“Yeah.”

“And got to stealing.”

“Aw, come on. Not that.”

“And I wanted to ask you if it was just a phase. Or is that you?”

“You know, I’ve thought about it myself.”

“And?”

“Well, at the time it just seemed everything we had had . . . except each other . . . had been stolen. And these kids, they thought it was fun.”

“Yeah?”

“And it was kinda fun. Kind of a game. Kind of exciting.” “And since then?”

“Well, I see it as a phase. Something I went through. I like making cookies better. And playing board games. And milking cows. And feeling useful. And wanted. And having a place of my own.”

“Yeah.”

“And parents.”

“Yeah.”

“So, is it done?” “Yeah. It’s done.”

“And when the summer’s over?”

“Back to school. Back to hitting the books. Back to playing sports.”

“And . . .”

“No more stealing. Haven’t taken anything since Lem got me out of that cabin I had climbed into up in Locklee. Don’t intend to.”

“Then I don’t need to tell Mom and Dad? You’re clean now. No need to worry them?”

“Nope. I thought about it. More than once. No need to worry them.” And he took down the claw from the cow’s udder as it had been released.

Jason left Marty to his milking and headed out to look along the rocky bed of the stream that ran not far from the house. He still loved nature and he figured what grew here would be different from what they had back east. So, he followed the stream’s sides to a rocky area where springs bubbled up in the water and picked up some pebbles and started skipping them across the water. And as he went to pick one up, he spotted a small, thin lizard that was grey, kind of silver. Black spots covered it. He bent to look at it. It didn’t look poisonous, but he decided to ask about it at lunch that day. And depending on what they said, he would return with a jar and see if he could capture it. When he left the stream, he headed back to the barn. He thought he would tell Marty about it. Maybe he would come back with him later and they might see if they could catch it.

Marty was brushing a cow. He was done with the milking.

“Finished, Marty?” The shade of the barn felt good. And he actually had come to not mind the barn smell.

“Yep. Done. What’s up?”

They walked together into the sunlight toward the house. “Well, I was down by the stream. There’s a rocky area with springs in it. Cool.

Pretty. And I was skipping stones there. And what do I see? A lizard. A long, thin lizard. Greyish with black spots. Didn’t look like any I’ve seen back home. I thought I’d ask about it at lunch and then, if they thought it wasn’t poisonous, I’d go back after lunch and see if I could catch it. Interested?”

“Oh, sure. . . after lunch. Right now, I’m ready to relax a bit. And eat."

* * *

Lunch was yummy. Leanora had made grilled ham and cheese sandwiches and a big salad with oil and vinegar on it. Large glasses of milk were beside each plate and a tray of homemade brownies sat in the middle of the table. Cal had returned from college yesterday, so a place was set for a fifth person. They washed up and sat down with Leanora and were soon joined by Bob and Cal.

Cal spoke. "How are you enjoying farm life, Jason?" "Oh, I like it. It's hard work but satisfying."

"You can say that again. How about you, Marty?

"Oh, I like it. And now that I have a real job, my plan is to save up and buy a new bike."

"So, you like taking care of the cattle? Milkin' the cows? Feeding them?"

"It's work. But it's good work." "How about you, Jason?"

"Well, driving tractor is a tough job. But I am happy to do it. There is so much to do."

"Yeah. I understand Dad taught you how to drive it. And he said you are good at it. And careful."

"Well, your dad is a good teacher. And what about you? How's college?"

"Just finished my junior year. One more to go. Majoring in animal husbandry."

"You like animals?"

"Yup. Always have."

"Say, do you know anything about a kind of a lizard I saw out by the stream. In the rocky area. It was slim and small. With small scales. Greyish. With black spots."

"Oh, them. They're called common wall lizards. Plenty of them out there. Fun to watch. I used to have one for a pet. A little female. You can tell the females because their underbellies and throats are white. The males are darker."

"I was wondering if it would be okay to catch one."

Leanora chimed in saying he would need a jar. She said she thought she had a good size one in the cabinet under the sink that he could have. Marty gave Jason a look and a nod.

"Oh, that'd be great!"

"When are you thinking of going for it, Jason?" asked Cal.

"This afternoon. Wanta' come?"

"Sure."

And so, it was the three of them had a plan for their first outing.

* * *

The sun was hot as they crossed the field to the rocky bed where the stream ran. Once there, however, the temperature was better and the trees along the rocky sides of the stream provided shade.

"Where'd ya' see it, Jason?" asked Marty.

"Over there by that large outcropping. It was almost the same color as the rock, but it passed over some lighter lichen and its movement caught my eye."

"Was it alone?" asked Marty.

"As far as I could see."

"Well, suppose we start with that same rock?" asked Cal.

"Good idea," answered Jason.

The three of them headed toward the rock. Jason climbed up the rocks near it. "I'll check out the top, you two check out the two sides and front."

Cal stood to the left, Marty to the right. The rock face was large, flat, and lichen covered. And just a bit back from its front face, it was embedded in the earth. The boys approach was thorough but turned up nothing. Then Cal turned back some ferns growing near the rock and low and behold!

"Look!" yelled Marty. And there under the fern was a mother . . . or was it a father? . . with a young one.

"How do we get it?" asked Marty.

Calvin scooped down with good speed and grabbed the larger of the two the sides of its head. "Like this!" he laughed.

Marty followed suit. And into the jar that Jason held they both went.

High fives all around; Jason would have his terrarium.

FIFTEEN Home Again but Soon to Leave

Late June 2019

Mary was in the kitchen and dressed by the time Lou came down for breakfast. He was still in his pajama bottoms and tee shirt. He came toward the stove to where she stood. He was smiling. He reached his right arm to hug her and then his left to seal the circle. She buried her head against his chest. It was such a nice feeling. Sleeping with him. Waking with him. Being hugged by him.

“Oh, Lou,” she mumbled into his chest. “Mary.”

And so, they stood a while. It was a long embrace.

“Well, Lou. I have to quickly eat my breakfast and down my coffee. I’ve made you egg salad for a sandwich so you can eat breakfast anytime. I think it best you not do any cooking while I’m not around. At least for now. Except for using the Keurig for making coffee.”

"You're probably right. What's for lunch?"

"There are cold cuts in there and I'll be home by four o'clock to cook dinner. And Carlos said he could stop by around lunchtime to say hello. And the OT will be here around one. Do you have a plan for this morning?"

"Well, I thought I'd read the newspaper and see if I can still do crossword puzzles. And maybe walk around the yard. And weed. And then after lunch, I'll watch TV for a while and probably take a nap."

"Wow! I'm impressed. The whole day planned!"

"It took me a bit. I cheated some. Wrote down a list of things I could do at home at the rehab and brought it with me. Then today, I decided to use it to help plan my day. Worked well."

"Yes, it did."

Mary noted as he sat down that Lou already had his watch on his left arm. He checked it for the time. "Maybe I will eat with you now," he said, and reached with it for the bread. Mary was impressed. He was doing his own therapy. He then held the package of bread in his left hand and took out two slices with his right one. He placed them on the plate in front of him and reached with his right hand for the egg salad. He had let his left hand go to his lap. With his right hand he scooped out some salad and moved it toward his sandwich.

"Your left hand, Lou."

"Oh, yeah." He laughed. "Forgot about that."

* * *

Carlos found Lou in the flower bed along the front of the Matters' house. He had a trowel in his right hand and was weeding with his left.

"Hey, Lou. How ya' doin'?"

"Hey, Carlos. Doin' well. Getting ready for OT. Practicing using my left hand. I'm holding the trowel in my right hand so unless I use my left one, no weeds are pulled. Seems to work. You wanna stay for lunch?"

"Well, I really just stopped by to say hello and find out if you need anything. Big day! Home alone. But Mary has been bragging about your progress and I'm sure you'll be fine. Anything I can do?"

"Nope. I'm fine. Wanna' come in?"

"Well, maybe for a minute."

Lou removed his right glove but forgot to remove the left one. They entered the house and Lou headed for the kitchen. "What about some coffee?'

"Sounds good."

Lou turned on the Keurig and when the lights went on, pushed the button for coffee. Whoops! What came out was water.

"Looks like I forgot to put in the K-Cup. Have to try that again."

Lou made two cups of coffee, the second one without omitting the K-Cup. He put out some cream and they sat together and chatted. Lou told Carlos about the Skyped conversation with the boys. Their visit was brief but pleasant, after which Lou made himself a sandwich and ate lunch. At one o'clock the OT arrived. He left at two and Lou sat to watch TV.

He had not tried the crossword puzzles.

* * *

Mary bought Lou a book of easy Sudoku and a book of word searches. They kept him occupied when he was home mornings. He continued to avoid using the stove or any power tools but did work in the garden weeding and did use the push mower. The sun was warm and bright on most days and he began to tan. He also gained a few pounds. And on Sunday night Lenore and Carlos would come over and they would play Scrabble, drink coffee, and snack. The weeks passed quickly. Lou was happy with the new arrangement and Mary managed the house, job, and transportation for Lou. It was tiring, but worth it.

And every Sunday they Skyped with the boys and Leonora and Bob. Jason was driving tractor and Marty had become an old hand at milking and caring for the cows. Both the wheat and the alfalfa had been harvested and the boys had been such helps that Bob was paying them seven dollars an hour. Marty was saving for a new bike and Jason for an Apple watch. School was closing and Mary and Lou had to make plans to go to Ohio.

* * *

The rehab had begun to look more foreign . . . less interesting. Lou was itching to come home for good and Mary was looking forward to the day when she had less transporting to do. Lou was still working on sequencing and double meanings and occasionally needed reminders to use his left hand, but his progress had been steady and both he and Mary were optimistic he would be able to leave the rehab permanently soon.

It was Monday, June 17, 2019. Mary and Lou returned to the rehab in time for supper there. Mary was tired, so they had headed out early. At the dinner table they were joined by the speech language pathologist. Her name was Becky. She was young. Not long out of college. But informed and pleasant.

"Hello, Lou. Hello, Mary. Nice you could join us."

Becky was seated next to a patient whose wrist she lightly held down between mouthfuls. The patient was new to them, but it was obvious she would have been stuffing her mouth and probably choking if Becky had not prevented her from using her spoon more frequently. Her food was pureed and lay in three different color pools on her plate.

"This is Sophie. Sophie is new here. Say hello, Sophie." Sophie gave them a mumbled greeting.

"So, Lou. Have you heard? They are going to dismiss you from your therapies."

"Really?"

"Yes. At the end of this week. After which you will be free to live at home. Of course, a nurse will check in on you weekly for a while. And OT will continue for a bit to help you with stove use and power equipment use. But I guess you are graduating!"

"Really? When?"

"They talked about Friday being your last day."

"Wonderful! Isn't it wonderful, Mary?"

"Wonderful! And school closes the same day! So perfect!"

Becky said they would have a special celebratory meal for the two of them on Friday after which they could say their goodbyes.

Mary was both thrilled and a bit intimidated. But they had come this far. They would be fine, she was sure . . . well, at least she hoped.

Mary's week was hectic at school, what with Individual Education Plan updates and some speech language evaluations to finish. And then picking up and returning Lou to the rehab center. But she made it. And come Friday she went straight away to the center to eat with Lou and bring him home. She found him already packed, his bag beside his bed. He was so excited; he could hardly eat. She on the other hand was only glad to sit down. Becky came by. And Lou's OT and old PT. And they had a cake for him which was shared with the other residents. It was clear to Mary that Lou was ready! His goodbyes were hurried by his excitement. She had not guessed how eager he had been to leave. But their goodbyes said, they wheeled him to the door as was their protocol at which point, he left the chair, picked up his bag and headed out to the parking lot, never looking left. Thankfully, there was no car coming.

Once in the car, Lou turned on the radio. He fiddled with the dial, found some country music, and settled back. They both rode in quiet until Lou asked, "When are we leaving?"

"Leaving. Oh, yes, leaving. Gosh, Lou, I've been so busy, it being the last week of school and all, I haven't even thought about it. And we have a lot to do before we go."

"Like what?"

"Well, I have to have the mail held and arrange for someone to watch the house."

"Oh, the house will be fine. Carlos with check it out on the week-ends, I'm sure. We just have to ask him."

"And the lawn. I need to arrange for it to be mowed." "Ricky can do that."

“Yes. I’m sure he can. But I need to arrange for him to have a key to the garage so he can get the lawn mower.”

“Just give one to Carlos. They can share it.”

“And, Lou, I’m tired. I need a day to rest. Let’s put off planning until tomorrow night. And just for this evening and tomorrow in the day, let’s just relax. Maybe we can figure it out to leave on Monday. After I talk with the mailman. After we plan our route. After we’ve made an overnight reservation.”

“We can drive through, Mary.”

“Lou, we can’t drive through. *I’ll* be driving and I need to rest after every hour and a half or so. As for you, you need to calm down. After all this time, we can take a day or so before we leave.”

“I can drive, too.”

“No, Lou, you can’t. It’s too early.”

“But I’m able to take care of myself fine now. And I can drive.”

Mary thought of Lou leaving the rehab center and how he had not looked left to see if a car was coming. No, he was not ready. And that was final.

“Lou. You cannot drive.” “Why not?”

“You would not be safe on the road.” She paused, “Sometimes you still forget to look left.”

Lou knew this was true. He also knew that he did not notice when he did not. He quieted. Mary would drive.

* * *

Friday night Mary just crashed, snacked on potato chips, and watched TV with Lou. Lou sat beside her on the couch. At times she took his hand and held it. She had decided to sit on his right side. No left side awareness therapy tonight. The school year had ended. Lou was home. The boys were safe with her sister. She was exhausted. Vegging out was real treat . . . and Lou beside her added to it. It would be so nice to have him beside her in the night.

“Tea, Mary?”

“Oh, nice of you, Lou. Just cream.”

Lou rose and went to the kitchen. Mary heard him clanging sink and kettle, getting out a mug. He returned in a few minutes. Tea was on. He sat beside her. Minutes passed; the kettle whistled. Lou rose and returned to the kitchen. With him he brought two mugs of tea. They sat together sipping it. Mary rose for a trip to the john. On her way, she glanced into the kitchen . . . just checking. The gas on the stove was still lit. No teapot on it. She turned it off and continued to the bathroom. Lou was home. He would need watching.

Lou was still a good sleeper, so Mary woke rested in the morning. Lou was up and at life as soon as she budged. He hugged her to him, and she accepted his warmth and kisses with gratitude and pleasure, but no lying-in bed today. There was too much to do if they were to leave tomorrow.

Breakfast passed peacefully. They ate in the kitchen where Mary could keep an eye on Lou as they jointly prepared breakfast . . . scrambled eggs, buttered toast, o.j., and coffee. Lou used the automatic Keurig with ease, even turning it off when their coffee was made. He helped set the table but placed most things to his right which was okay as they could sit adjacent to one another, kitty corner at the table. Usually they sat opposite one another with everything in the middle of the table. Well, it looked like that was changed. No problem. Mary doubted Lou noticed she was seated.

Again, she had sat herself to his right, so she knew she was in his view.

“So, Lou, I was thinking that after breakfast you might use MapQuest and print out our route to Springfield. Once we are there, I know my way to the farm so no need to do that detail.” Would he be able to do that? He’d been using the computer to search for the boys.

“Good idea. And after that, I help pack.”

Mary was glad he had some sense of sequence for the day. As much as it was a help to be a speech language pathologist, it did add to one’s awareness of progress, lack of progress. But he was doing well. Just still needed supervision.

“And, Lou, we need to find a place to stay the night on Monday. Ten hours of driving is too much for one day.”

“Okay. I’ll find a place about three hundred miles out.”

They cleaned up the kitchen and Lou went to the computer. Mary pulled two overnight bags from the hall closet and carried them to their bedroom. She placed them on the bed, opened them, and began to pack both her own and Lou’s. The toiletries they would put in tomorrow, but the underwear, jeans, shirts, socks, and Lou’s work boots would go in now. As she packed his shirts, she selected only tight-fitting ones. She knew the risks of wearing a loose fitting one around the machines on the farm. Yes, Lou around the farm machinery. She just hoped they were between harvests. She thought they would be. She remembered other Junes in Ohio and recalled only the lettuce being ready. And maybe some early cukes.

Sounded safe. And maybe Lou could help in the barn with the animals. Probably pretty safe . . . just the risk of running into things on his left side. Or forgetting a sequence and not being able to work the milkers. Well, enough of those thoughts.

In the den, Mary found Lou had made good progress. He had used MapQuest successfully and was printing out their route. On it he had determined they would put up in State College, Pennsylvania. That would mean driving four and a half hours the first day and more than six hours the second. Way too much for Mary. Then it occurred to her that Lou was planning on driving, too.

"Lou, hon. The route is fine, but I'm going to have to stop sooner. The second day is over a six-hour drive. And I can't do that."

The expression on Lou's face was one of shock. He understood. He would not be driving.

"But Mary. Out there on the open highway, I'll be fine."

"Lou. You don't know that. There are still times when you neglect your left field of vision. You did it this morning when you set the table for breakfast. Why do you think I sat beside you rather than across the table from you?"

"You wanted to . . ."

"Well, I did. But that was not the only reason." "Then why?"

"Because you set the table facing its side and put all the things to the right. I would not have been able to reach them from the other end. They were not in the middle."

Lou thought a bit. "I get it. I didn't look to my left. Did I?" "No, you didn't Lou."

And so, it was agreed that Mary would drive, and they would stop two nights on their way to Springfield. So, Lou went back to the computer and Mary sat beside him and with some prompts from her, they agreed to stop once in Williamsport (Billtown as it was known) and once in Youngstown, Ohio.

Mary suggested finding places to stay in the center of the towns so they might walk around and look at the area and maybe eat outside the hotels. Lou was amenable to that and so together they selected the TownePlace Suites in Williamsport. It was a Marriott, but its prices were reasonable. And in Youngstown, which they knew to be a city that was in the rustbelt and with a struggling economy, oddly they found the hotels nearer the center of town were all booked for single rooms with double or queen-sized beds so they settled for a Best Western a bit to the south of Youngstown in Poland, Ohio. Both hotels' rates included breakfast which meant probably a serve yourself continental one with a quick getaway each morning which they liked.

Sunday went slowly. Lenore and Carlos and Ricky and Steven came by in the afternoon for brief visit. Ricky who would be turning fourteen soon had grown considerably and Steven, who was six going on seven stuck to his older brother's side, hanging on to his every word. Carlos and Lou went outside to sit at the picnic table behind the house and the boys followed along.

"How's Lou doing, Mary?"

"Well, on the one hand he is doing wonderfully. On the other, he really can't be left alone."

"Why not?"

"Well, he still is not seeing things to his left consistently. Bumps into things with his left shoulder. Doesn't duck if something comes toward that side of his head. Keeps thinking he is up to driving. Planned the trip so that we would drive more than six hours on one day . . . assumed he would do some of the driving. I had to iksnay it. But he accepted it. At least for now.

"But on the positive side, his sense of sequence has improved. He had been using it regularly in the search for the boys. As a result, this morning he was able to use MapQuest on the computer. Except he planned to drive as he did so.

"But he misses things. Like this morning. Made tea and left the burner on when he was done. Nothing happened yet it's a warning sign of forgetfulness."

"How will he be in Ohio. On the farm. They have tractors and lots of farm machinery, don't they?"

"Yes, but it is between harvests and I think the only thing to pick is lettuce and maybe some young cucumbers."

"But what will he do all day out there?"

"Well, I will explain to my sister and everyone there how he cannot be left alone. So, he can help my sister in the kitchen and do things like sweep down the porch. And maybe go to the barns mornings."

"What would he do in the barns?"

"Well, I suppose he could help feed and clean the animals . . . and maybe he might be able to learn to use a milker. I understand the boys do."

"Well, Mary. I wish you the best. It can't be easy."

"It has its moments. But he is home and lucid and not particularly defensive. Which could have been a major problem."

"And what do you hear from the boys?"

"Well, Jason has learned to drive a tractor and helped with the harvest. And Marty has become quite a milker. Goes out every morning and evening to help. And I guess they wander the stream that is near the house. And play cards. And both are saving the money they earn. Jason for a laptop and Marty for a bike, I think. We talk to them by Skype. They look wonderful. The farm has done them well. Both have built muscles and are tan. And Jason has really grown taller."

SIXTEEN Together Again

Summer 2019

Monday morning rolled in early. Lou and Mary were up at the crack of dawn. They put their bags in the trunk of the car and after Mary talked with the mailman, they were on the road in no time. Lou had the MapQuest directions stuck in the side pocket and they each had a covered coffee mug in the center stash. As the sun was behind them most of the time, they didn't need sunglasses.

Mary had had the car checked out on Saturday. The tank was full. They were ready. First stop would be for eggs and coffee near Moscow, PA. As it was ten when they left that would be around noon. From there they would get to Williamsport, PA, a bit before noon, check into the Williamsport Marriot where they had reserved a room, shower, and head out lunch. After lunch they would go for a cocktail in an area pub and head back to the room to rest. And when it was cooler . . . after four thirty, they would walk around the town before dinner. After dinner they would return to the hotel, wander around, and return to their room to watch TV. And early to bed. For the rest of the trip, the plan was the same except on Tuesday they would stop in Falls Creek, PA, for a break and bunk down in Youngstown, Ohio, and on Wednesday they would stop at Mansfield, Ohio, and end their trip in the afternoon on the farm outside Springfield, Ohio. The MapQuest trip plan was nine pages long. Lots of sequencing practice for Lou, but the bottom line was that the car had a GPS in it and Lou would need to use the MapQuest printout only if he so chose to use it to talk about where they were going next or how long it would take to get there with referring to the GPS.

On the printed sheets, Mary had starred the stops and to mark the end of each day on the MapQuest guide sheets, she had drawn frames around the overnight stops. By so doing, the list was broken up into three shorter lists and they were all stapled together in the upper left hand corner. Whether they used it or not on the trip was of little import. It had been a great help in trip planning . . . and surely good practice for Lou.

Moscow was a tiny town of a couple of thousand. Its main claim to fame was it having a railroad station. They had breakfasted outside of town and their timing was off, and it was a bit after noon when they hit the town's center, so they opted for brunch at the Olde Brooke Inn. Lou ordered a couple of slices of sausage and pepper pizza and Mary had a hamburger with a salad. The food was tasty. They thanked the waitress and were on their way.

The skies remained clear as they pulled into Williamsport, a pretty town that bragged of its history as the Birthplace of the Little League. They checked into the Best Western and as it was still early, they dropped off their bags and headed out. 'Billtown' was filled with lots of art and artists. Lots of old Victorian charm. They stopped at a small pub, passed time in the bar restaurant area of the hotel, took a nap, ate dinner, walked the streets some more . . . Mary always on Lou's left side . . . , returned to their room, showered, and watched television before bedding down early, happy to be together again.

Mary texted her sister.

"Hi, Leanora,

All is well. We are in Williamsport. Youngstown tomorrow night. Then Springfield and see you all come Tuesday late. Hope the boys are behaving.

Lou sends his regards. Love and hugs, Mary"

Day two to Youngstown with brunch in Mansfield went well. Mary and Lou talked. They talked about their time apart. Their boys. Now. But of the future, nothing was mentioned.

All in good time.

Youngstown, Ohio, was in not the best of conditions. Its economy had been affected by the decline in the steel industry. But Lou and Mary stayed at the Best Western in Poland, just outside of Youngstown and it was fine. They were happy just to sit around and talk or just share a quiet moment. Mary was looking at Lou. Lou was looking out the window.

"Lou. I've been thinking. First about how well you have been doing. Second of some weakness you still exhibit . . . in left side awareness. In sequencing . . . although that really seems to be near normal. For instance, you seem to be comfortable with the Mapquest printout of our trip plan and can use it to refer backward and forward to trip distances and markers. And you have shown some forgetfulness. Like not turning off the burner after you made tea at home."

"Yes. You should have known me when I first came out of the coma. I had amnesia. Didn't even know my own name. Could not sequence hammering a nail with a hammer to build a bird house. Forgot there was even life to my left."

"Yes, I'm aware of that. And I wish I'd been there for you. But you managed well without me. And the main thing is your marvelous progress. And your disability stipend will not run out before December. So, my question is, what will you do when it is done?"

"Well, the Plant is no longer a possibility." "No."

"And I still have some weaknesses."

"Yes." Mary admired her husband for his courage in seeing and being able to state that.

"So, I may not be able to drive. And I may not be able to work with electricity and machines with moving parts."

"No."

"But I have been thinking of retraining."

"Yes. But as what?"

"As a website designer."

"What a grand idea!"

"I could take courses at the community college for starters. They told me at the rehab that while I was receiving disability benefits, I might also get some job training. Also, they would help with placement when I am ready. I would need a lift back and forth for classes, but the disability program would also provide that except as the college is on your way to Aesopolis maybe sometimes you might take me. Or maybe, once I am in the classes, I could find someone with whom to share a ride."

“Oh, Lou.” Mary went to stand before him. She raised her arms and placed them round his neck. “You are so wise. I love you. You make me happy.”

* * *

Continental breakfast and then off by nine to Mansfield for lunch and in the evening, Springfield, and Mary’s sister’s place. And seeing the boys! Mary’s sense of anticipation was almost palpable. Lou seemed calm and pretty much in the present.

Around eleven they pulled into Mansfield, Ohio. The temperature was comfortable, in the seventies.

Mansfield was an old town and like most rust belt cities was pulling itself up from loss of manufacturing. But because of its location, the railroads were an important part of the economy. Two attractions they passed were the Ohio State Reformatory and the Carousel. The former was no longer in use and had fallen to disrepair within, but its outside was an impressive castle-like gray stone building with turrets and towers. As they looked for a place to lunch, they realized the town’s thriving arts community included a symphonic orchestra, a ballet company, a dance company, and the Mid-Ohio Opera! For a city of fifty thousand, impressive.

As they had come in North Main Street, they found parking there and went to the Coney Island Diner . . . located in a large brick front building but with the old diner style decor . . . lots of aluminum and plastic topped counters and tables and a diner style menu.

“Hmm,” said Mary. I think a Reuben is what I would like. You?”

"I'm thinking I would like to try the meatloaf sandwich with fries and slaw. Haven't had meatloaf in a while and haven't had a meat-loaf sandwich since I was a child."

Back on the road Mary sensed Lou was also anticipating their arrival on the farm. He referred frequently to the MapQuest travel guide, changed the station on the radio more than once, and talked more than he had in days.

"Can't wait to see the boys!" "Me neither."

"They seemed so much more mature when we talked with them on Skype."

"Yes. Both of them. I'm sure they have many stories to tell. And I wonder how much it took for Jason to keep Marty on the straight and narrow."

"Well. Looks like he did. And that's what counts."

They pulled up before the house around two o'clock. It was quiet. No one in view. They got out and walked up the steps leading to a large porch. Behind the screen door, the front door was open wide.

"Leanora? Bob?"

Down the stairs at a near run came Marty. "Mom! Dad!"

He had burst through the screen door not knowing who to hug how first. But he settled on his mom and his dad waited his turn. His dad noted how Marty had grown. He was almost as tall as Lou was.

Leanora came from the kitchen. Apparently, she and Marty were the only ones in the house. But about then a truck pulled up and out came Cal, Jason, and Bob. They approached the house steadily, Jason in the lead.

"Mom! Dad!" He, too, had grown and was now taller than Lou by a couple of inches.

The boys got the suitcases from the car and carried them up to the second-floor bedroom where Leanora and Mary awaited them. Then they all headed downstairs and settled in the kitchen where there was iced coffee and iced tea for all.

"Hey, Dad. Jason has a mother wall lizard and her baby. Some people call them geckoes."

"Nice. Where's he keep them."

"In a jar."

"Know what we feed them?"

"Bugs?"

"When we catch one. They like crickets. But we feed them mealworms. Leanora had some she found growing in an old box of cereal. Except we don't have a lot. So, we will probably take them back to the stream in a couple of days. But for now, they're interesting."

"I'm sure they are."

"Cal had one when he was a kid, so he showed us how to pick them up. You know how?"

"By their tails?"

"Well, you could, I suppose. But Cal's way is by the head. You hold it between your thumb and forefinger, like this, and let their front legs go between the rest of your hand. Except they are getting tame now and will walk onto your hand."

"Maybe later you can show me."

“Except you have to wash your hands with soap and water when you are done. Salmonella. You know.”

“Sounds good to me.”

* * *

Lou and Mary talked about the trip out and where they had stopped along the way and what they had seen. They talked about Lou in rehab and his return to home. They talked about their search for the boys and the happy day when Leanora had called them with the news they had been found.

Jason and Marty filled Lou and Mary in on more details of their travels and eventual rescue and coming to Springfield.

But Lou was tired and needed a nap and the cows needed to be milked and Leanora needed to start dinner so the family gathering disbanded, each going their own way, leaving Leanora and Mary alone in the kitchen.

* * *

“Let me help you clean up here, L’nora.”

Leanora gave her sister a hug. “I can’t tell you how happy I am to see you! And Lou seems to be doing well.”

“He is. Still, I need to talk about not only his progress, but his weak areas.”

“Yes. Do.”

“Well, as you know, Lou suffered memory loss, except it seems to have repaired and returned. And he had difficulty with sequencing things. That seems to be almost gone. And he doesn’t get irony. He has difficulty inferring second meanings. Like when he first came home, I jokingly said to him, ‘Not too happy to have you home!’ to which he responded, ‘I thought you’d be pleased.’ But that doesn’t usually cause any major problems. However, he does have two weaknesses that still interfere and at times cause risk. One is, he forgets . . . like to turn off the burner when he is done cooking. And the other is his left side neglect.”

“How does that present?”

“Early on, he could see but as his left field of vision in both eyes was gone and did not recognize that he was not seeing things on his left side. Right side brain injury sometimes causes that. And as the left side of each eye doesn’t process left side vision, it is like being blind to things on the left. Unless he moves his eyes to scan to the left with his right field of vision.”

“So, watching for cars crossing the street would be a problem?”

“Yes. And especially so because he forgets he doesn’t always see things to the left. I mean it is better, but it is not like he sees things there one hundred per cent of the time.”

“So how does he cope with that?”

“Well, that’s it. In a way he can’t as he doesn’t know what he does not see . . . and does not remember to look for things on the left by turning his head or the direction of his gaze. His field of vision has improved as he scans to the left more with his right field of vision than he had been, but his awareness remains a bit spotty.”

“So, what do you do?”

“Well, he accommodates. I accommodate.”

"How?"

"Well, take the trip. He can't drive as his ability to see traffic, buildings, and signs on his left is unreliable. So, I drove. Luckily, he is reality based and non-macho enough to have accepted that."

"So that's it?"

"No.

"When we walk, I walk on his left side. It prevents him from bumping into things and people."

"Oh."

"And most of the time I sit on his left side to encourage his increased awareness of it. In the beginning, I would have to touch his arm to get him to look at me. And put the knife in his hand so he would remember it. Or turn his plate so the left side became the right side, and he would see that side and eat the food on that side, too."

"And what happens when you are not there?"

"Well, he sometimes will bump into the doorjamb. Or if there is something hanging at head height, he might bump into that."

"Oh, my goodness. In the barns, that could be a problem." "I know. And that's why he can never be left alone."

Leanora's response was silence. This was something to contem-

plate. After dinner that night they were all sitting around in the living room. Bob wanted to know more about Lou's injury. "So, in the explosion, you were thrown against a wall and hit your head."

"Yeah. I don't remember it, but however I hit it caused right side brain damage."

“Then what happened?

“I don’t really know. At least I can’t recall what happened. Whatever it was, it put me in a coma for a day or two and when I woke, I had severe amnesia. Didn’t even know my full name. That’s why Mary was never contacted and told where I was. But then of course she had her own problems.”

“Yeah. We know about her radiation sickness.”

“Thankfully, it passed. That was just about the time I recalled my name and they could let her know where I was.”

“How’dja find out, Mary?”

“A telephone call. They told me that Lou was at a rehab to the north of our home. I went to see him there. He was in pretty rough shape. Couldn’t sequence things to do such things as simple as get out his shaving cream, put it on his face, shave, rinse, and dry. He’d get the first part right and then forget to rinse or dry. So, the speech language pathologist worked on sequencing with him. And OT had made a bird house that he could put together if he used the correct order. Luckily, he was able to read the instructions in order.

“Also, he couldn’t see anything with the left half of his eyes’ field of vision or on his left side. That is an aspect of left side neglect and it is caused by right side brain injury. So, you might sit beside him all evening and if you were on his left side, he’d never see you and the next day he wouldn’t remember you as having been there. With time and practice his attention to his left side will improve, but not necessarily the left field of vision in his eyes.”

Leanora had already heard this, but Mary explained it now to Bob. “And he couldn’t understand words as having more than one meaning. Or irony. So, when I said to him, ‘Not too glad to have you home!’ he thought I meant I didn’t want him there. We got it straightened out, but that aspect of language still bothers him. And while his sense of sequence seems fine now, he still has vestiges of left side neglect, so he can't drive as he might miss seeing things . . . even vehicles . . . on his left side.

"And for instance, sometimes he will bump into a door jamb with his left shoulder. And downstairs in the basement, I had some flowers hanging from the ceiling to dry, and he turned his face right into them. Never saw them as he approached them."

"So how do you keep safe, Lou?"

"Well, Mary's been wonderful. Partly because I don't even see these weaknesses . . . until after the fact. So, when we're out, Mary stays on my left side. And I have agreed not to drive. At least not while the neglect is still in evidence. And I'm even going to change professions. No more work in the Plant for me. Nope. I'm going back to study web design."

Quiet filled the room.

Bob spoke. "Well, you know the early harvesting is done now so we aren't using tractors and big machines except for the trucks. And for now, mostly we just keep the vegetable garden weeded and watered. And care for the cattle. Maybe tomorrow you might go with Marty and me to the barn and you might help us with the milking. Wadaya' say, Marty?"

"Sounds good to me."

"And we'll just have to make sure one or the other of us always keeps your dad to our right."

"Yup. We can do that. Wadayathink, Dad?" "Sounds good to me."

* * *

The men and boys were up early, but Lenora and Mary slept in until around eight. Jason went off with Cal someplace on the farm and Bob, Lou, and Marty headed for the barn. Marty announced he would stay on his dad's left side. "That okay, Dad?" Lou mussed his hair and gave him a smile.

Lou had never milked a cow, so Marty directed his dad to sit down on the spare milking stool. Bob left with a caution to Marty to call him if he needed him. He would be cleaning nearby.

Marty demonstrated the use of the claw. "Now, Dad, before you milk, first you have to wash off the cow's udder and especially her teats with this iodine." He demonstrated how.

"Next you put the plug in the milker so it will form suction. Then you put the milkers on the teats, front to back, right side, front to back, left side. They just hang on of their own accord and release when the milking is done." Marty demonstrated, sitting beside his dad on the second stool as they waited for the milkers to release. "Okay, now. Another dose of cleaning with iodine and we're done."

They moved on to the next cow. "Okay. This time you help, Dad."

He gave his father an iodine-soaked rag to clean off the udder, taking it from him when he was done. Then he gave his dad the hose with funnel on its end to dip each teat in. Then he asked his dad to again sit while he demonstrated the use of the milkers. And on the third cow, after his dad had cleaned the cow's udder and teats, he asked him to apply the milkers.

His dad put the first milker on. It did not hold.

"Dad. What holds the milker on the teat?"

"Suction."

"What causes the suction?"

“Well, the pull of the machine up the hose.”

“Yup. But what makes the pull go all the way to the teat?”

“Suction.”

“And can the hose have a hole in it?”

“No.”

“Well that hose has a hole in it.” Marty pointed to the place where the stopper went in.

“Oh. I forgot to put in the stopper.”

Marty slapped his dad five! And after that, unless his dad was sitting, with Marty always on his dad’s left side, the milking went well.

* * *

Marty and Lou were waiting for Bob so they could head back to the house and clean up.

“Hey, Dad, why don’t cows have any money? Lou just looked at him.

“Because farmers milk them dry.”

His dad thought a bit. “I think most cows have milk left when the farmer is done.”

Marty looked at his dad. It occurred to him his dad just didn’t get it. He thought he’d try another. “Hey, Dad. What do you get when you cross a cow and a duck?”

His dad just looked at him with a puzzled expression.

"Milk and Quackers! You get it, Dad? It's a joke. Quackers. That's what baby ducks are. They quack. So, they're quackers. So, when you mate a cow and a duck you get milk from the cow part and quackers from the duck part. Isn't that funny? It's a joke."

Lou didn't laugh, but he confirmed he had understood. "Yeah. Cows give milk. Ducks hatch quackers."

"Is that funny, Dad."

"Yeah. That's funny."

But he didn't laugh.

Mom was right. His dad didn't get the second meanings.

Maybe in time.

Maybe with practice.

Marty and Lou were on their way to the barn. They had just passed Cal going by on a tractor. Marty thought he would try it again. "Hey, Dad, stop. Know how the farmer got his wife?"

"No. How?" His dad looked at him as if he really expected an explanation.

"He tractor down." His Dad just stood there, looking expectant. "Yah, get it, Dad? . . . Tracked her . . . tractor? You know, looked for her, tracked HER, tracTER?"

Lou's face showed a light. "Hey, that's a good one. Tracked her . . . tractor . . . a farmer, eh?" He gave Marty a hug and they went on their way, the low moo of cows in the barn beckoning them.

Leanora and Mary were preparing dinner. That morning they had weeded a bit in the garden and brought in fresh lettuce and cilantro from it. Tonight, they would have Wild West beef hash. Mary peeled and cut up seven potatoes and browned them in oil in a rather large skillet, moved them to a large bowl, and set them to the side. Leanora put out some homemade salsa and a Bell jar full of corn kernels that she had canned the previous fall and prepared a half cup of chopped fresh cilantro and two cups of shredded Cheddar cheese. Then she gave Mary a couple of pounds of beef to brown and salt and pepper in the same pan as she had browned the potatoes. When the beef was brown, Leanora stirred in the salsa, corn, and cilantro and after a few minutes, added the potatoes. And when she was done, Mary spread the Cheddar over the top and Leanora mixed it in until it melted after which they put it in the oven to keep warm. When the men and boys returned in a bit, they would transfer it to two large and colorful ceramic pie plates, and pour some sour cream over them and sprinkle some of the fresh cilantro over them, leaving only the salad to prepare. They set the table together.

Two sisters. It was not the first time they had worked together to prepare a meal and the process had a comfort level about it.

The house was quiet. They had worked with minimal talking. Leanora cleared her throat. "Mary, I've talked with Bob and we've been thinking that maybe it would be good for Lou to stay with us come September when you go off to work."

"Oh, Leanora!"

"Yes. Well, we were thinking that he gets more physical exercise here than he would in Ariana. And he's not ready to go back to work. He still misses things on his left side. And he is only beginning to make more frequent conversation. And Marty says he's only beginning to get jokes."

"But that is so much responsibility. Back home we would have the therapists come in . . . at least one a day . . . and he wants to learn about how to build websites . . . he recognizes he is not safe around electrical work . . . so we could have a tutor come in to work with him. Or rehab could help us find a program for him."

"Well, it's an offer. No strings attached. And he is a help . . . with the milking. He could work with Bob or one of the hands when they are in the barn. Cal will be back in school, so he won't be available. And maybe there is some online training Lou could take. For building websites. You know."

* * *

The dinner was fun. The men and boys were hungry and thirsty. They drank their milk or coffee with their meals. Everyone enjoyed the shredded beef and cheese casserole. Most took seconds. A salad balanced things as a lighter side. And there was blueberry pie to follow.

"Hey, Cal. Did you hear how the farmer got his wife?"

Cal gave Marty a quizzical smile. "No. How did the farmer get his wife?'

"He tractor down."

"Oh, yeah? You think that's cool, huh? Well, then tell me how the farmer found his lost cow."

"I don't know. How did the farmer find his lost cow?"

"He tractor down."

"No, fair, no fair. That was my line."

"Too bad. You missed it." Even Lou laughed at that.

It was Jason's turn. "What type of horse only goes out at night?"

Lou was into it. "What kind of horse go out at night?"

But Cal knew the answer. "Nightmares!"

"Get it, Dad?" asked Marty. "Bad dreams. NIGHT mares?"

"Oh, yeh. I got it. Nightmares. A mare is horse. And a night mare is a horse at night. Also, a bad dream." Lou looked proud.

Mary and Leanora gave one another knowing looks: Lou was on the mend.

* * *

Mary and Lou were alone in the bedroom getting ready for bed. "Lou, you seem happy here."

"I am. Leanora and Bob are the best. And Cal sometimes works with me when I am milking . . . to give Marty more freedom . . . and they all watch my left side. Also, I think my left side awareness is improving."

"But not enough to return to driving, right?"

"Not enough to return to driving. Just today I ran into a light bulb hanging right to the left of my face in the barn. Didn't see it. But I felt it. It was hot!"

"And not ready yet to return to work. Right?"

"Not yet. Still get the sequencing of things confused. Like I still forget at times to put the plug in the milker before I go to attach it to the udder. But it is happening less often."

"So, Lou, what do you think you should do when I go back to school in a week or so?"

“Well, I guess I could still get some therapy at home. And maybe find some online course on website building.”

“Or maybe stay here for a couple of months with Leanora and

Bob?”

“Oh, that’s too much to ask.”

“Well, I guess it isn’t. Leanora brought it up to me while we were preparing dinner today. I told her it was too much, but she said that she and Bob had discussed it. Cal will be back in school, and you could help with the milkings. If Bob or a hand is with you.

“Let me think on it. I mean I would miss you. And I would miss the boys. But it is an idea. And I can help with milking.”

* * *

When morning rolled round, Lou woke Mary. He was on his way to the barn, but he seemed excited.

“Mary. I’ve thought about it. I think my staying here for a month or so is a good idea. When I am in the barn with Bob, I will talk to him about it. And I will let you know at lunchtime.” He bent and kissed her, she smiled at him, and rolled over and went back to sleep. It was still dark outside.

* * *

At lunch when Lou and Bob returned, Bob walked down the path with his arm across Lou’s shoulders. They were both smiling.

"Hi, Leanora." Lou gave her a hug. Much in the style the old Lou might have done. They washed up and everyone sat for lunch.

Lunch was ham and cheese sandwiches, salad, and chocolate cake.

"How come I like ham and cheese so much?" asked Marty.

Cal answered. " 'cause you're a ham and your jokes are all cheesy."

"Now is that nice?" laughed Marty and gave Cal a hit to his arm. "Maybe you like it, too!"

"Good one!" responded Cal.

Lou looked serious. "I have something to tell you all."

The boys looked at one another. What was this? Their dad so serious. And starting a conversation. More like their old dad. "Bob and I have been talking. Right, Bob?"

"Right."

"And we have come to a decision." "Yes, we have."

"Bob and I have decided I am going to stay here in Ohio for a few months while you boys and your mom go back home and start school."

"You're staying here, Dad?" asked Marty.

"Yep. Going to help with the milkin'. And take an online course in website design."

"How long ya' staying, Dad?" asked Jason.

"Oh, a couple a' months. Maybe 'til Thanksgiving."

"And Leanora agrees to this?" Jason looked at his dad and then at Leanora.

"Yes. We've all talked about it."

"And your mom and I talked about it before I went to the barns this morning. It was a hard decision, but I think it is for the best. I can't drive yet, and I am not ready to return to my old line of work. But I can help here. And while I do, I can keep getting better. And maybe by Thanksgiving, I'll be all well. And possibly ready to do web design."

"Oh, Lou, I think that is wonderful! It will be nice to have you here. Cal will be at school and it will be nice to share meals with you. And I am sure Bob can use you in the barn."

"Well. It's a little sudden, Dad, but I think it's a good idea," said Jason.

"Yeah, I agree," chimed Marty. "And Bob can tell you jokes so that by Thanksgiving you get them more easily. Maybe easily. After all, you're the one who taught me to tell them in the first place."

"Well, Lou, we'll miss you so much," said Mary. She rose to give him a big hug and continued talking. "But we can facetime. And the fall goes quickly as starting the new school year is always a bit demanding. And we can see if the rehab can help us if need be when you return. And who knows? Maybe by then you will know enough about websites to begin to contract to do them."

Inwardly, Mary and the boys breathed a sigh of relief. They would miss Lou, but the boys had catching up to do at school and Mary could use the break. Thinking ahead Mary decided that the only thing left to do was to pack and make the return trip. She decided they would follow the same route that they had used in coming, stopping five times on the way. It would be fun. She thought they would leave on Monday, in time to settle in and shop for school. That would give them the weekend to say their goodbyes. And to pack.

Mary thanked goodness for her kind and generous sister and brother-in-law and son, for surely, despite the upside of Lou's help in the barn, it would be a responsibility. And only time would determine how it would all work out . . . time and patience. But they had survived. And they were still a family. And in some ways so much of it seemed so far in the past.

EPILOGUE BY LENORE

Dear Reader,

As Mary's best friend, it had become my plan that once Mary Matters had become stable I would take it upon myself to find out just what exactly had become of her sons, Jason and Marty, that fateful day in April 2017. As at the time I made the plan, it was still possible they had been kidnapped by the terrorists. And somewhat less likely, it was that they had been killed or wounded and hospitalized by the blast of a dirty IED. However, as I had learned that the specificity of the family's escape plan was well known to their older son, Jason, it was my guess that as the house was some thirty or thirty-five miles from Magdum Heights, it was more likely the boys had fled north as they said they would and were well and healthy despite their whereabouts being unknown. So, it became my plan to nurse Mary back to health and then help to find the boys. Of their father, so near as he had been to both The Plant and the majority of dirty bombs, neither Mary nor I had held out much hope.

April 12, 2017 being the date on which The Plant went down . . . I know I said April 11 in the first printing of *Jolt: a rural noir*, but I was still confused—and all those fires set and dirty bombs strewn about in such a way as to cause all that endless confusion, fear, and much fleeing of the area—some of which it was later determined might have been unnecessary. But then with the grid down and communication so poor, who was there to correct the misinformation and calm the fears of the people? And of course, there was the approximately seven-mile land radius around The Plant where radioactive levels were high due to the spinoff of fission from The Plant. And there was also severe contamination of the James River south of the plant caused by the leakage of the radioactive materials from not the plant so much as from the pools that cooled the spent radioactive waste. In fact, dirty bombs had confused the findings to the extent that they had significantly raised ground level radioactivity in spots as far as thirty miles north and east of The Plant. Very confusing.

I say this because we now know that in the first day or so after the events, radioactive materials had been carried hither and thither on the feet of unwitting bystanders who in their ignorance fled the scene with radioactive materials on the soles of their shoes. Thus people repeatedly tread through the radioactive matter deposited from the numerous dirty bombs that had exploded and spread it about in such a way as to cause the uninformed to believe that given the meltdown at The Plant, there must have been invisible fallout from The Plant that had contaminated every inch of the surrounding area up to some fifteen or more miles. Yet much of the calamity could have been lessened had the general populace understood that while radioactivity is not visible to the naked eye, fallout, it being an ash, for the most part was. Well not, of course, the fallout from Chernobyl by the time it reached America, its radioactivity already degraded, and its density reduced to other than such that the casual observer would say it was still visible. But at that time, as Mary and I were colleagues, albeit in different schools, and she a speech language pathologist and I a special education teacher, and as Mary was in no shape to travel, one Saturday when Carlos was home, I headed north to Bain to find her sons. But we failed and it was not until much later, after the boys had been located and the family united that through working with the Red Cross there, it was explained to me how the boys had survived, thanks to their wits and a call from a man named Lemme who lived in North Country in lakeside town named Locklee.

Then a year and a half later, with Mary apparently continuing to stay well and Lou recuperated and working in website design and advertising, Carlos and our boys and I, in looking for a new place to vacation, set out for Locklee to enjoy the mountains, lake, and sun . . . and I, in the hope of meeting the man, Lemme, who had found boys. This in turn led me to meeting and talking with the Locklee residents, including that handsome dog Thaw with his scarred arm and magnificent painting style, as well as Natalie, at the time newly pregnant but still deeply involved in community affairs and planning. But probably it was Martha who gave me the best of leads and given her background as a librarian and natural researcher, it was she who helped me most in weaving into whole cloth the story of all those wonderful characters I wrote about in *Jolt: a rural noir*. Except in *Jolt*, to be honest, I changed their names to those used in this book and presented them, too, as fictional characters when in fact, they were not. However, for me the challenge was to conceal their identity as well as my own as it was not possible for me to really know the exact words in which they had communicated, nor, of course, could I have known with certain accuracy all the details of their survival on the shores of Locklee Lake. Oh, I suppose I might have researched it all further, but enough is enough, and my main interest then as now was just to write a good story. And so, where the bits and pieces were missing, I simply made them up of whole cloth in such a way as to permit them to serve as story glue wherever necessary.

Of course my telling you this story was indeed quite different, for, as I said, Mary Matters and I were friends and so part of the tale I have told you I lived through with Mary, and happily, Mary lived through it, too. Of course saying this at this point, may be of only tangential interest to you the reader, however, so rather than belabor the point, I believe it best to just quiet my pen and hope you have enjoyed *Two Close: A Story of Survival* and look forward to its sequel, *Coming Back*.

Lenore

Roberta M. Roy has lived most of her life in the Mid-Hudson Valley in New York State. The destruction of the Twin Towers in New York City on 9/11/01 encouraged her to take a hundred hours of direct instruction from the military in how to respond to mass emergencies. Her studies culminated in the week-long CBRNE course in Bethesda, Maryland in which the emphasis was on how to respond to chemical, biological, radiological, nuclear, and high yield explosive mass events. Some of the less theoretical information she garnered from that course and others, as well as from research into alternative waste management, housing alternatives, and intensive gardening has found its way into the story of the Magdum Heights meltdown survivors and responders as they struggle to bring their lives back to normalcy.

Roy is the recipient of a 2011 Jenkins Living Now Awards medal in Inspirational Fiction and a 2020 Jenkins International eLit Award in Poetry for her book, *Poetry by Roberta M Roy, Slivers*. She is also the author of the sequel to *Jolt: a rural noir*, *Two Close: a story of survival*; *Straight from the Robin's Nest*, a collection of essays on a variety of timely topics; and *The ALVA Axiom Anthology of Author Interviews*. Roy holds a B.A. in English from the State University College at Albany and an M.A. in Speech-Language Pathology from the University of Nebraska, a Certificate of Clinical Competency in Speech-Language Pathology from the American Speech-Language Association (ASHA) and a license as a Speech-Language Pathologist in the State of New York.